MISSING YOU

"I'll miss you guys," Meg smiled. "It'll be hard to have a good time without you."

Now Stevie and Laura both laughed as Stevie said, "Try, Meg. Try real hard." At that, all the girls burst into their familiar giggles as the talk turned to what Meg was actually going to need to bring with her to Kansas.

Stevie had it all figured out. "All you'll need are cowboy boots, a saddle, and a nice, slow way of saying 'Howdy,' " she joked.

Suddenly realizing the real fact that she *was* going to Kansas to see Molly and meet The Terrible Three, Meg shook her head thoughtfully as she said, "Something tells me I'm going to need more than that. A lot more."

P.S. We'll Miss You
Yours 'Til the Meatball Bounces
2 Sweet 2 B 4-Gotten
Remember Me, When This You See

REMEMBER ME,
WHEN THIS YOU SEE

Deirdre Corey

AN
APPLE
PAPERBACK

SCHOLASTIC INC.
New York Toronto London Auckland Sydney

To my real friends forever,
Louise, Pam, Eunice, Leslie, and Mom

ISBN 0-590-42624-9

12 11 10 9 8 7 6 5 4 3 2 1   0 1 2 3 4 5/9

Printed in the U.S.A.   40

First Scholastic printing, August 1990

FRIENDS FOREVER
FORGOTTEN

Looking out her bedroom window, Meg Milano could see all the way up to the corner of Doubletree Court. The leafy branches of the giant maples and oak trees that lined the street somehow parted at just the right spots to allow Meg a perfect view. She was watching to see when her friends Laura Ryder and Stevie Ames would finally round the corner and make their way to her house for the Friends 4-Ever Club meeting. They were a few minutes late, but Meg knew she could count on them to get there soon.

As she stood at the window, Meg could see

the brightly colored striped hammock hanging between two trees next door. For as long as Meg could remember, the hanging of the hammock signaled the beginning of summer. One week ago, right on schedule, the hammock was suddenly there, and so was summer.

Through a crisscross of spreading branches, Meg saw another familiar sight. It was the open gate leading to the backyard of two elderly sisters. The two women made it a habit to welcome the neighborhood cat, Cookie, for a free meal at their back doorstep. The always-opened gate allowed Cookie to eat and run whenever she chose.

That gate was as important to Meg as it was to Cookie. Meg liked things she could count on. She liked seeing the hammock every summer. She liked seeing the gate open every day. And she liked what she saw when she took another peek through a jumble of leaves on a middle branch. Coming down the street were Laura and Stevie.

Now, like a queen in her ivory tower, Meg looked down on the two subjects who were walking fast and laughing as they tried to outdistance each other. They had no idea that Meg was watching them being so silly. Stevie was squatting down, her long, reddish blonde hair falling forward as she took large steps. As she walked, she pumped her arms forcefully. She was just getting ahead of Laura when Laura suddenly took three ballet leaps forward and left Stevie behind. Next, Stevie stood up straight and just plain ran past Laura, giving Laura's long brown hair a flip as she raced by and reached Meg's door first. Laura turned her walk into a pretty ballet dance, ending with a deep bow on Meg's doorstep. Both girls were giggling wildly when Meg went downstairs and met them at the door.

"You guys are really funny to watch." Meg laughed. "Walking the way you were walking, it's no wonder you're late!"

"You saw us?" Stevie giggled. "Where were you?"

"In my room, looking out my window. I can see everything from there," Meg explained.

"Everything?" Laura asked.

"Even all the way to Kansas?" Stevie joked.

"Wouldn't that be too good to be true," said Meg. "If I could do that, I'd be able to see what Molly was doing every second of the day."

"That *would* be too good to be true," Stevie agreed.

"And wouldn't it be great if Molly could see us, too?" Laura added dreamily.

"Yeah. Then she would have seen you dancing down the sidewalk two minutes ago in your crazy way." All the girls laughed at that idea. Molly would have laughed, too, if she had been there. The sad fact was that Molly Quindlen wasn't there and had been gone for almost a whole year. None of the four friends would ever forget the day on which Molly announced the horrible news that her family was moving to Kansas. Molly's grandfather was ill and unable to run the family hardware store, Quindlen's Hardware Store, in Cross Plains. The store had been in the Quindlen family for three generations. Mr. Quindlen felt he had no choice but to move his family so that he could run the store until his father was up to it again. Molly understood and so did the other girls, but understanding didn't stop the tears and the sadness. The four girls had grown up together and had done everything as a foursome. Now that they were separated, they still kept their friendship going strong through the Friends 4-Ever Club. Letters

4

flew back and forth between Crispin Landing, a neighborhood in Camden, Rhode Island, and Cross Plains, keeping the girls in touch and up to date.

"Well, anyway," Meg interrupted the laughing, "are you ready for the meeting? Let's go up to my room." Just as she was turning to lead the way inside and upstairs, a familiar voice called out to them.

"Rainbows in the mail today!" It was Ed the mailman delivering a pile of mail to the Milanos' box. He handed Meg the stack of magazines and letters and held out a big, fat envelope decorated with rainbows.

"A letter from Molly!" shouted all three girls together.

"Perfect timing," Stevie said. "Now we can start the meeting with Molly's letter."

Ed handed the letter to Meg and walked off whistling. "Wow," said Meg, bouncing the letter up and down a little in the air. "This is a fat one!"

"It's probably full of all the good news about her coming home soon," Laura guessed. "Can you believe it's almost a whole year since she left?"

"I wouldn't exactly say it went speeding by," said Stevie as a way of reminding the others how much she had suffered with her best, best friend gone.

"Well, at least she'll be back with us by the end of the summer," Meg said. "I can hardly wait."

"Open the letter," urged Stevie as they stood on Meg's doorstep.

"Not until the meeting is officially called to order," Meg teased. "Come on up." Laura and Stevie followed their leader up to her room. As they went in, a flash of orange fur rushed past them.

"Marmalade!" Meg shouted, as her cat darted past and bounded down the stairs.

"Nice seeing you, Marmalade," Stevie joked. "Sorry you couldn't stay for the meeting." Laura and Meg laughed as they usually did at Stevie's brand of humor. Meg was already in her room, tapping the small gavel on her neatly organized desk. That was Meg, always in charge, always neat.

"The meeting is now officially called to order," she said.

"Finally," added Stevie.

"Go ahead and read," Laura said excitedly.

Slowly and dramatically, Meg opened Molly's rainbow-covered letter. Before it was even all the way out of the envelope, Meg could see the word "Boo-hoo" written all across the page. Molly had made the o's into eyes with giant teardrops falling from them.

"Uh-oh," Meg said worriedly.

"Uh-oh what-oh?" Stevie asked.

"I don't know yet," Meg answered. "Just listen." She unfolded the two sheets of paper and began to read the most important letter Molly had ever written to them.

Dear Stevie, Meg, and Laura,

This is the hardest letter I've ever had to write to you. If you see smeared ink on the page it's because teardrops are falling onto this letter. I guess I'd better start at the beginning. About a week ago my parents were doing a lot of talking about when we'd be coming back to Crispin Landing. I overheard them saying stuff about packing and sending things home. My mother was talking about all the extra stuff there would be to send, since I have all the horseback riding things now. My room is full of riding things. My mother says it looks like a stable.

Anyway, when she started talking about sending my things home I started realizing what it all meant. It meant I was moving again. It took me a while to make friends here, but now I do have real friends and I get to ride my friend Kristy's horse, Chocolate, every single day. Going home would mean I wouldn't see Chocolate anymore. I didn't understand how I could be having sad feelings about moving back to my real home. But I did feel sad.

Last night I heard my parents talking again. But this time they weren't talking about going home. They were talking about not going home. Grandpa's doctor says Grandpa is not ready to take over the hardware store yet. He doesn't feel strong enough to go back to work. The doctor said these things take time. Now I am having different feelings. Now I am crying because I will not be coming home at the end of the summer after all. Now I will still have my friends here and I will still have Chocolate. But I won't have you, my best, best friends in the whole world. My feelings are all mixed up. I wish I could see you, and now I don't even know when that will be. Don't forget me. No matter how long I'm gone we have to stay,

Friends 4-Ever,

Molly

P.S. Remember me when this you see
Rainbows forever!

When Meg finished reading, no one said a word. Meg slowly folded up the letter and then looked at Stevie and Laura. Stevie sat on the rug, looking down and playing nervously with one of the pieces of fringe on the edge of it. Meg could see that teardrops were falling from Stevie's cheeks to the floor, but Stevie seemed not to notice. She just kept twisting and twisting the piece of fringe.

9

The teardrops in Laura's eyes hadn't quite started to roll down her pretty face. They puddled up like pools in her eyes. When at last she blinked, the tears took their tumble. Meg wasn't crying. She was too stunned and surprised at the words she had just read. Then, as she looked at the tearstained faces of her two close friends, the real meaning of the news hit her.

"I can't believe she's not coming back," Meg whispered. "It's not fair!"

"I already have my calendar marked with the countdown of days until she was supposed to come home. It was only going to be fifty-five more," Laura whispered, too.

Stevie still sat silently. She wiped her eyes with the shoulder of her T-shirt. Her finger was completely wrapped in the rug fringe and there were red welts where it had been circled too tightly. Slowly she unwound the fringe loop and finally looked up at Meg and Laura. "Even fifty-five days was too much for me," she said. "How will I ever stand it without Molly?" More tears trickled across the freckles on Stevie's face. Stevie almost never cried. Laura immediately put aside her own disappointment and put a comforting arm around Stevie.

Meg understood just how Stevie felt. They were all going to miss Molly even more than they already did, but Meg could see that Stevie felt she would miss her the most.

Whenever there was a problem to be solved it was Meg who usually did the solving. If the girls went exploring and came to a split path, Meg was the one to step forward and say, "This way, gang!" If a pet wandered off and was nowhere to be found, Meg would lead the search and come back with the lost animal. When Molly announced the news of her move to Kansas, it was Meg who saved the day with the idea of writing letters back and forth and having the Friends 4-Ever Club. Now Molly's latest and most unhappy letter ever presented Meg with the biggest problem she'd ever had to solve.

"I haven't figured it all out yet," announced Meg, matter-of-factly. "But something has got to be done. We can't stay apart from Molly any longer than we have to."

"The trouble is, we do have to," said Stevie, sadly. "And the other trouble is, I'm not so sure she even wants to come back to us. You heard what she said about that dumb horse and her new friends out there."

11

"I understand what she means, though," said Laura, remembering her own experience of making friends with Shana, a girl who was not in the club. "We're allowed to have other friends, right?"

"Well, sure," said Meg, "as long as they're not better than the best."

"To me," Stevie said quietly, "Molly is the best best."

"And that's exactly why I'm going to find the best best solution to the biggest problem the Friends 4-Ever have ever had," Meg announced.

Stevie and Laura just stared at Meg. They'd seen that look on her face before. It was Meg's look of determination. It was clear that Meg had made up her mind to do something about this terrible mess.

"Trust me," said Meg. "Just trust me." And they did.

PLANS

Meg was certain of it. Molly was in trouble and Meg was the one to help her. Molly had said her feelings were mixed up. Meg knew the best way to help her unmix them was to make sure she knew how her real friends from her real home felt about her. The last thing the girls had done at the meeting was write their letters to Molly. Meg had all three letters spread out in front of her, ready to fold up and put in the mail.

She read them over one last time, starting with Stevie's letter written on her special club stationery with the bright blue high-top sneakers at the top of the page. Next to the sneakers Stevie had drawn a picture of a rainbow with a big stew pot at the end of it. In the pot was a stick figure of a girl. Stevie had written the name Molly and drawn an arrow pointing to the figure in the pot. Meg laughed as she began to read.

Dear Molly,

That's supposed to be you stuck in a stew pot at the end of the rainbow. I guess what it really should be is all four of us in the pot together, since we're all in this big mess together. But why do I feel like it's more unfair to me than to everyone else? I guess it's because you are really my best friend in the whole wide world. If you're not coming home at the end of the summer, like you were supposed to, when are *you coming home? And when you come home will you feel like you're leaving home, too? Don't answer that. I don't think I want to know. What I do want* to know is how am I going to stand having you there and me here?

You never have to worry that I will forget you. I'm more worried that you'll forget me! I only wish we could see each other now. From the way you sounded in your letter I don't know if I should be happy for you that you don't have to leave that horse, or sad for you that you won't be here for all the great Crispin Landing celebrations (like the Fourth of July Parade that's coming soon). I am sorry for me, though, because I miss you, Molly. Write back soon.

Yours 'til the windowpanes are cured,

STEVIE

Next was Laura's letter, written in her delicate handwriting on her special stationery decorated with unicorns:

15

Dear Molly,

I really understand how you feel. It must be terrible to have your whole life so mixed up right now. You know we all cried when we read your letter. We couldn't believe that you would have to stay there longer. I know you must have felt so sad when you thought you were leaving all your Kansas friends and, of course, Chocolate. And now you feel sad that you won't be with us, but you should try to feel happy that you have friends both places. We won't forget you. How could we? You are what makes the Friends 4-Ever 4-Ever. Without you it would be 3-Ever, which doesn't sound nearly as good. We will just have to write more often, that's all. But I wish we could all be together again soon.

Love from your faraway friend,

Laura

And last of all was her own letter, which she read again just to make sure she'd said everything she wanted to say.

Dear Molly,

Your letter was the saddest one we've ever gotten from you. We were all so excited about you coming home to us at the end of this summer. I already had it all planned for what we would do at the first club meeting with you back. It was going to be a big welcome home party, and after the party we were going to go over to your house and help you set up your room exactly the way it was before you left. I know you would want everything to look just the same as it was. Since we all spent so much time in your room, we would all remember where things went. Then, once you had your real room back, your feelings wouldn't be so mixed up anymore, I'm sure. And once you had your old friends back, and

I do mean us, we would all be happy again. But Molly, don't worry. I know everything seems too too terrible right now, but somehow, some way, I am going to think of something to do to make things better. I'll let you know my plan as soon as I have one.

Your friend 4-ever,

Meg

"As soon as I have one," Meg said aloud. Suddenly she felt the burden of the promise she was making to her friends. They would all be counting on her to do what she did best, fix things. But how? She had to think, and think hard. Meg pulled out Molly's letter again, hoping to get a clue from it as to what she should do to help her friends. Reading it a second time, Meg could hardly believe it.

How could Molly feel sad about leaving *them?* she wondered. Meg remembered what Molly's letters said when she first moved to Kansas. In the beginning, the same kids Molly now said she would miss were mean to her. Three girls in particular ganged up against her just because Molly had made friends right away with one of their friends, Kristy. Molly called the mean girls The Terrible Three. They did sound pretty bad from Molly's descriptions of how they always showed off riding their horses, how they were allowed to ride into town by themselves, and how they even hung around with boys!

I guess maybe they're not as terrible as they used to be, Meg reasoned silently. But what Molly needs now is "The Terrific Three," namely Stevie, Laura, and me! Meg's eyes lit up.

"Or maybe *just* me!" she said out loud excitedly.

Suddenly the perfect plan started to form in her mind. Of all the plans you've ever had, Meg Milano, she thought excitedly to herself, this has got to be the absolute best!

In fact, she couldn't believe that she hadn't thought of it the night before when she heard her parents talking. They had been talking "business," as they often did. Usually Meg tuned it all out. But the night before her ears perked up when she heard her own name mentioned. They were talking about possibly taking Meg with them to a convention of science writers. Because Mr. Milano flew so often, he had earned some free plane tickets. They could use one of them for Meg, and maybe she'd enjoy seeing what a convention was all about. Meg's father and mother talked and talked about it, and finally decided to think it over a little more. When she heard that, Meg figured there was no need for her to get excited yet. Since they were still thinking, it might not even happen. Now Meg realized that since they were still thinking, she just might be able to put in some ideas of her own.

Leaving the club letters on her desk, Meg ran downstairs to get something out of her father's study. She came back to her room, carrying an atlas. Sitting on the floor, Meg turned to the map of the United States. Her eyes carefully followed the states between Rhode Island and Molly's new home state of Kansas. Making as straight a line as possible with her finger, Meg traced over Rhode Island, Connecticut, New York, Pennsylvania, Ohio, Indiana, Illinois, Missouri, and finally Kansas. She reached up to her desk and pulled down a plastic ruler. The distance measured between Rhode Island and Kansas was eight and a half inches.

That's not too far at all, Meg thought. And there are no if's, and's, or but's about it. I'm going to visit Molly! Having decided it as a fact,

Meg decided to go down and talk with her mother about this. Feeling happy, she took two steps at a time and landed on the bottom with a jumping thud.

"Are you all right, Meg?" asked her mother, coming in to see what happened.

"I'm better than all right," Meg replied. "I'm great! I'm fabulous! I'm incredible! I'm — "

" — up to something," Mrs. Milano finished for her. "The last time I saw you like this, Miss Meg, we ended up with a neighborhood carnival and pet beauty contest in our backyard. What should I expect to find here this time?" Her mother smiled as she teased Meg.

Meg got right into it. "Well, it's not exactly what you'll find here," she explained. "It's more what you won't find here. Well, what I mean is, what I *hope* you won't find here is me!"

"What's that supposed to mean?" her mother asked curiously. "And just where will I find you?"

"Hmmmm," said Meg thoughtfully. "Maybe Kansas?"

"What?!" Mrs. Milano said with great surprise. "What are you talking about?"

"Me visiting Molly," Meg started carefully.

21

"Aw, Meg," her mother said gently. "I know how disappointed you are to find out the Quindlens aren't coming home yet. We're all sad about that. But you going to Kansas? That's just not possible. You'd have to fly alone. You might not even be allowed to fly alone at your age. Not to mention the cost of flying."

"But I heard you and Daddy talking about free plane tickets. Why can I have the free tickets to go to some silly convention, but not have them to do the most important thing I've ever had to do in my whole life? You don't understand. Everyone is counting on me." Meg was getting close to tears. She could see her whole plan falling apart before it had even begun.

Mrs. Milano put an arm around Meg's shoulder. "Oh, Meg, you really are something." She sighed a big sigh, smiled slowly, and said, "Well . . ." It was the "well" she always said when she was giving an idea serious thought. Meg felt encouraged.

"Well?" she prodded her mother hopefully.

"Well," said her mother again. "We'll have to talk it over with Daddy. And we'll have to call the airlines to find out the rules. And of course we'll have to call the Quindlens and see what they would think of all this."

"But you're not saying no, right?" asked Meg hopefully.

"We'll see," said her mother. "Tonight we'll discuss it with Daddy. That will give us all a little time to think about it."

"I don't have to think about it," said Meg. "I already know what I want."

"That's for sure, Meg Milano," her mother agreed. "You always do."

Meg didn't hear her mother's last words. She was already up the stairs and pulling out a pen to add one more thing to her letter to Molly.

Meg couldn't help but smile as she wrote, *P.S. Help is on the way!*

BITTERSWEET

It was a perfect day in Crispin Landing. The sun was bright in the clear blue sky. A soft summer breeze blew through Stevie's long, reddish blonde hair and Laura's long dark hair as the two girls rode their bikes up and down Half Moon Lane. Stevie's favorite bike trick was lifting both feet off the pedals, leaning back, and throwing her head back so that her hair flew out behind her. Laura did bicycle ballet, pointing one toe out to the side and lifting the other leg up parallel with the bike's wheels. Half Moon Lane was Stevie's street and it was also Molly's.

Now, as the two girls rode back and forth past the house where Molly had lived before moving to Kansas, they called out "Hi, Molly!" every time they reached her driveway. Anyone passing by might have wondered what in the world it meant when they heard, "Hi, Molly! Hi, Molly! Hi, Molly!" again and again. In fact, Mrs. Hansen, the elderly woman who'd rented Molly's house, did open the door to call to the girls.

"Good morning!" she said. "Isn't it a beautiful day?"

"Hi, Mrs. Hansen," called the girls together. They didn't stop pedaling. They couldn't. Their legs were going too fast now. Stevie was ahead of Laura, so far ahead that she had already turned around and was coming back toward Laura. She slowed down as she got near her.

"What's the matter," asked Laura, noticing the sudden change in Stevie's expression.

"Guess," said Stevie, coming to a stop at the edge of Molly's driveway.

Laura pulled up next to her. "Molly?" she asked.

"I just can't get used to the idea that she's not coming back yet," explained Stevie. "And I keep thinking about her liking those new kids as much

25

as she likes us. If I moved away I'd never get used to the new place, and I'd definitely never let other friends take the place of my best friends."

"It isn't like that, Stevie. It couldn't be," Laura defended Molly.

Stevie knew Laura was probably right, but that didn't change the fact that she felt miserable without her good friend . . . and that she was jealous. Stevie flipped her hair back over her shoulder and threw her leg over her bike. Turning her handlebars in the direction of her own house two doors down, she said, "Let's go to my house. I guess we better start doing what we planned to do today."

Laura followed, happy to have Stevie change the subject. "Yeah," she said, "we have a lot to do before the parade." They were both talking about one of their neighborhood's biggest events. The Crispin Landing Fourth of July Parade allowed everyone to take part in the making of the "floats," which were really just cars decorated with streamers. The younger children dressed up in tricornered hats and carried American flags. The older kids decorated their bikes and rode together as the parade marched up and down all the streets and courtyards of Crispin Landing. There would be music and refreshments for all. At the end of the day the whole neighborhood gathered at the park for a big picnic supper and fireworks. It was an event no one would want to miss, and one the girls had always worked on together.

Stevie pulled into her driveway and got off her bike. Laura pulled in beside her, hopped easily off her bike, and gently nudged the kickstand down. Her pink-and-white bike glistened in the bright sun. "Where do you think Meg is?" Laura wondered.

"Don't worry about Meg," Stevie said. "She knows we're meeting here to get our bikes all polished up. I talked to her on the phone last night."

"So did I," said Laura. "But only for a minute. She had to get off because her parents were expecting an important phone call."

"We can start polishing without her," Stevie said, turning to pick up an old rag and some chrome polish. She handed Laura another rag and noticed that Laura's bike really didn't need polishing at all. It looked brand-new even though Laura had gotten it last year. Laura started polishing anyway.

"The parade isn't going to be so much fun this year," Laura said as she rubbed an invisible speck of dust off the pink back fender. "This will be the first parade without Molly. I just realized that."

"I already thought of that," Stevie said, as she rubbed extra hard on her scratched chrome handlebars. Her bike was not pink and it did not look new. It had belonged to her older brother Dave and then to her middle brother Mike. Now it was all hers. It was blue in spots where the paint had been scraped off by falls and crashes. And it was exactly the bike Stevie wanted.

"Hey!" said Laura, trying to cheer them both up. "I've got a great idea. We should do a special club theme when we decorate our bikes this year. Something that shows we're all still together, even if we do have to be separated."

"Like what?" asked Stevie, looking interested. "What kind of theme?"

"Well, like how about a Friends 4-Ever theme? We'll all decorate our bikes with the same color streamers and have a banner that goes across all three of our bikes." Laura stretched her arms out to demonstrate how the banner might go.

Stevie got caught up in the excitement of the plan. "Yeah!" she said enthusiastically. "And it could say, 'Friends 4-Ever — Molly, Stevie, Laura, and Meg!' "

"What about Meg?" Meg asked as she surprised the two girls by pulling up on her pink-and-white bike.

"Where've you been?" asked Stevie, waving the rag in the air. "We've been here for hours already. And we've even planned the whole bike parade. So there."

"Without me?" Meg protested. "Hey, that's not fair!"

"We didn't really plan the *whole* thing," Laura began.

"We weren't trying to leave you out," Stevie said. "You just weren't here. And Laura came up with a great idea. Tell her."

Laura excitedly described her idea to Meg, but in the middle of her explanation she realized that something was the matter with her friend. "What is it, Meg?" she asked. "If you don't like that idea we could do something else."

Meg was quiet for a minute. "No. It's not that.

29

It sounds like a great idea. It's just that, well, I have some good news and some bad news."

"What do you mean?" Stevie asked, looking at Meg suspiciously.

"Well, it's not exactly good news, it's more like great news. But the bad news is that I won't be able to be in the parade this year." Meg waited for their reaction to her shocking statement.

"Not be in the parade?" Stevie gasped. "Why not?"

"Meg, what do you mean?" Laura added.

Meg hesitated. "Remember the day we got Molly's letter saying she wasn't coming back?"

"Yeah," said both Laura and Stevie together.

"And remember I said trust me? That I'd find a way to fix things?" Meg could see the girls were confused but curious.

"Well, I *am* going to fix things. I'm going to make sure Molly doesn't forget who her *real* friends are. And I'm going to help cheer her up about not coming home."

"How?" Laura asked.

"What are you going to do, kidnap her and bring her home?" Stevie laughed.

"No," said Meg slowly. "But I am going to do

30

something incredible. I thought and thought about what to do and then I realized that what Molly really needs is us with her. And since we can't all be with her, and since my parents have free plane tickets that I can use, and since the Quindlens said yes, well . . ." Meg took a deep breath. "Well," she said again, "I'm going to Kansas to see Molly!"

There. She had finally gotten the news out. There was no way she could put the words back in her mouth. But as soon as she looked at Stevie's face and then at Laura's face, Meg suddenly wished the words could be taken back. She had known they might react a little funny at first. But what came next she never expected at all.

"How could you, Meg Milano?" Stevie sputtered angrily. "If *anyone* should go see Molly it should be me. I'm the one who's really her best friend. *I'm* the one who really misses her most. It's *me* who cares more about Molly than anyone else does." Stevie's freckled face was red and her fists were clenched.

Now Laura got into it. "That's not true, Stevie. We all care about Molly. We *all* miss her. She's everybody's friend. If anything, we should *all* be going."

Meg stood holding her breath and feeling afraid. Everything was getting spoiled. The night before all the calls had been made. The airline had said she could fly alone. The Quindlens said they'd love to have Meg. And Meg's father had agreed she could go, since he had the tickets anyway. Meg had been happier than she'd ever been before. She felt that she had done what they all expected her to do — figured out how to solve the problem. What she now realized was that there was a new problem. Her friends were jealous and angry, and now all three of them stood in Stevie's driveway glaring at each other. Stevie was the first to leave the group. She turned and ran inside her house, slamming the door behind her.

Meg's shoulders heaved up and down as she sobbed and said, "I was only trying to help. I never meant . . ."

Laura felt sorry for her friend. She went over and hugged Meg. "I know you were, Meg. I'll talk to Stevie. Don't worry. It would've been great if all of us could have gone. But it's still great that at least one of us can go. I'm not mad, Meg."

"Stevie will never speak to me again," Meg

cried, holding on to Laura. If Meg had looked up she would have seen another tear-streaked face watching her from inside the house. Stevie saw Laura putting her arms around Meg. She saw Meg crying uncontrollably. She saw Meg hugging Laura. And the next thing Meg saw was Stevie slowly opening the front door and coming out to the driveway.

Meg ran over to Stevie. "Oh, Stevie," she said sincerely. "I'm really sorry. I wanted to *fix* things, not make things worse. I was only thinking how great it would be for all of us if I could go there and be with Molly so she'd remember us and see that *we're* the ones who are her best friends. I won't go. I'll tell my parents I'm not going."

Stevie wiped her own tears away and silently hugged Meg. "You're going," she finally said. "Of course you're going. I won't be mad. I'll wish it were me, but I won't be mad."

"I'll miss you guys," Meg smiled through her tears. "It'll be hard to have a good time without you."

Now Stevie and Laura both laughed as Stevie said, "Try, Meg. Try real hard." At that, all the girls burst into their familiar giggles as the talk turned to what Meg was actually going to need to bring with her to Kansas.

Stevie had it all figured out. "All you'll need are cowboy boots, a saddle, and a nice, slow way of saying 'Howdy,' " she joked.

Suddenly realizing the real fact that she *was* going to Kansas to see Molly and meet The Terrible Three, Meg shook her head thoughtfully as she said, "Something tells me I'm going to need more than that. A lot more."

PACKING

"Mom?" Meg called down from the top of the stairs outside her room. No answer. "Mom?" she called again, louder this time.

"What is it, Meg?" her mother called back finally.

"I don't know what to pack." Meg went back into her room and opened all of her dresser drawers. Then she opened her closet door. Her big blue canvas suitcase lay open and empty on her bed.

"I'll never figure out what to put into this thing," Meg said disgustedly at the suitcase. As if on cue, Marmalade chose that moment to jump up onto the bed and climb over and into the high suitcase. He walked in a circle for a second, then settled softly into a corner.

"Great!" Meg laughed as she pretended to close up the suitcase. "Marmalade, you're all I'll need, so now I can just close up this thing and forget about it." Marmalade sensed the top of the suitcase coming down and jumped out in a flash right before it closed over him.

"Don't worry, you silly cat," Meg giggled. "I was only joking." She opened the suitcase up again, and its emptiness stared back at her.

"Mom?" she called again.

"Just bring the things you'll need," Mrs. Milano called back helpfully. "I'm sure they dress the same in Kansas as they do here."

"Oh, right," said Meg under her breath. Packing was not easy. Meg had packed a lunch box before. She had packed an overnight bag for sleepovers before. She had even helped pack her own suitcase for her family's yearly summer visit to their cottage on the lake in Massachusetts. But when they went to the cottage it was only for a week. Most of the stuff she needed was already at the cottage since they left "cottage clothes" there from year to year. She'd never had to pack from scratch. And she'd never had to pack for a two-week visit to a place she'd never been before. She took a deep breath and looked into her closet for a third time. It was organized perfectly, of course, so it was easy for Meg to see what she had to choose from. She didn't have a lot of clothes — Meg had always taken pride in the fact that she always picked clothes she really liked a lot and didn't mind wearing often.

She pushed a couple of hangers aside and looked her things over. First there were the blouses and skirts hung together in outfits. She saw her jean skirt paired up with a red-and-white-checked blouse. Next was a pink-and-blue-flowered blouse hanging with a blue layered skirt. And last was Meg's favorite outfit, the one she called her "every occasion outfit." The top was a purple-and-white-striped sleeveless blouse and the skirt was solid purple. This outfit also had purple shorts to go with it and a purple cotton cardigan that came down halfway over the short skirt. Meg pulled this outfit off the hangers and laid it on the bed next to the suitcase. She looked at it thoughtfully. Then she folded it up and put it in the suitcase.

"There," she said, satisfied.

"Where?" Stevie's voice asked. Meg had been so lost in her thoughts that she hadn't heard Stevie and Laura walk up the stairs and into her room.

"Hey!" Meg laughed, surprised. "How'd you get in here?"

"The door," answered Stevie.

"Me, too," added Laura. "We thought you could use some help getting your stuff all together for the trip."

"Could I!" Meg said, shaking her head. "I'll take all the help I can get. This is impossible. I don't have any of the right clothes for Kansas." Meg held up her favorite purple outfit. "Even this doesn't seem right."

"I love that outfit," said Laura, defending Meg's choice.

"So do I," added Stevie, "but you're right. It's not right for Kansas." She went over to Meg's open drawers and started taking out stacks of plain shorts and tops. Then she took out a pair of jeans and a sweatshirt. Arms loaded with Meg's clothes, Stevie hurried over to the bed and dumped the big bundle into the suitcase. "There you go," she said matter-of-factly. "Done. That's all you need. The purple is too much of an outfit or something. What you want is just plain stuff, nothing so fancy."

"So is that it?" Meg asked.

"That's it," Stevie assured her. "The packing is over."

Meg and Laura laughed at Stevie's fast-packing technique. "I don't believe you," said Meg. "Here I've been, standing around for over an hour, trying to figure out what to bring. Then you come in and do it in two seconds."

"Hey," said Stevie, slapping Meg on the back a little too roughly. "That's what friends are for, right?"

Laura had gone over to the top drawer of Meg's dresser and pulled out a summer night-gown, some pajamas, socks, and underwear. "Don't forget this stuff," she said. "I'm sure they wear underwear in Kansas."

"Probably longjohns." Stevie laughed. "That's what the cowboys always wear in the movies."

"Yeah, and they all drink out of tin cups and cook beans around the campfire, too, but that doesn't mean that's the way it is in Kansas to-day," Meg said, sticking up for Molly's new home just a little bit.

"Well, just remember why you're going," Stevie reminded Meg.

"To save Molly from the clutches of The Terrible Three and The Kids From Kansas!" Meg said dramatically.

"Somebody save *me!*" Stevie said, wincing at Meg's overly dramatic performance.

"Here's some other stuff you need," Laura interrupted. She unloaded an armload of hair ribbons, barrettes, Meg's kitten stationery, extra sneakers, a pair of jellies, another pair of jeans, and a picture of all four girls together. Laura placed everything in the suitcase except the picture. Handing it to Meg, she said, "Just so you don't forget *us* while you're out there."

Meg looked horrified. "I'd *never* forget you! Ever! How could you even say a thing like that? And if for some horrible reason that did start to happen, then you two would just have to figure out how to come and rescue me!"

"Are you kidding?" asked Stevie. "And have to pack two more suitcases like this one? No way!"

"Help me close this thing, will ya?" Meg asked her friends as she struggled to push down the pile of clothes enough to zip the case. All three of them pushed and mashed and squashed and squished the bulging suitcase. At last they won. It was closed. The top looked a little lumpy, but at least everything was in it. Breathless, the three packers collapsed to the floor all in a row and leaned back against the bed.

"Whew!" gasped Stevie. "I guess you ought to have enough stuff in there to last a while."

"Wait!" said Laura worriedly. "We forgot one thing."

"How could we have?" asked Stevie. "The only thing she isn't bringing is the cat!"

"But she's not bringing *us*," said Laura seriously.

Stevie rolled her eyes upward. "Let's not start *that* all over again," she said. "We can't all go, and that's just the way it is."

Meg could see that Laura was thinking of something else. "What do you mean, Laura?" she asked.

"Some 'N' Stuff put together especially for Molly, by us," explained Laura. "Each of us has to choose one very special thing. Something that will remind Molly of each one of us. Each thing has to be a real treasure," Laura said dreamily.

"She's right," Meg agreed. "We'll take turns.

You go first, since it was your idea, Laura."

Laura thought hard for a minute. Then her eyes lit up. "I know! The last picture Molly sent of herself showed she didn't have bangs anymore. She'll probably be needing more barrettes." Laura reached up to her own hair and removed the twin-hearts barrette she was wearing. "I'm sending this to Molly to remind her that our hearts are always with her."

Meg knew how special Laura's gift was. The twin-hearts barrette was her very favorite one. It would be hard to choose something as special as that. Meg needed more time to think. "You go next, Stevie," Meg said.

"All right," said Stevie, reaching deep into her pocket and pulling out a small, sparkly, turquoise superball. "That's easy!" She gave the ball a good bounce. Even on a rug the ball bounced so high it hit Meg's ceiling. "This superball is to remind Molly to come back to us." Stevie bounced the ball again and caught it. "See, just like that."

"Perfect," said Meg, holding out a small box for the ball and the barrette. And then Meg did the strangest thing. She opened her desk drawer and looked around until she found a pair of scissors.

"What are you doing?" asked Laura curiously.

Meg walked over to the mirror hanging over her dresser. Draped over the mirror frame were all kinds of mementos from wonderful times. There were blue and white streamers from a great soccer game, paper flowers from the class play, and a string of paper hearts from a Valentine's Day party. Even with all these souvenirs of important events covering much of the glass, Meg could see enough of her own face to know what she was doing. She stared thoughtfully at herself for a minute. Then carefully she held out one of her longest, blondest curls. With scissors in one hand and the fat curl in the other, Meg snipped her hair off. One perfect blonde curl snapped into a loop around her thumb and index finger. Laura and Stevie both gasped and stood watching with their mouths open.

"There!" said Meg proudly, holding up her prize present. "I'm putting one of my curls in the box because Molly has always wished she had my hair. Now she'll have it!" She wrapped the curl in a piece of her kitten stationery, wrote

43

the date and her name on the paper, and added it to the box.

"I can't believe you did that," said Stevie with great admiration in her voice. "I can't believe you really did that!" Stevie had always thought she was the only one in the group who was at all daring. Meg had just proved her wrong.

"That was a beautiful thing to do, Meg," Laura said softly. "That is the best treasure of all."

The girls closed up the box, and Stevie and Laura hugged Meg. Tomorrow she would be flying high above the rooftops, carrying the box safely to Molly.

To Meg, the idea of being in Kansas at this time the next day was as strange as the idea of being in the Land of Oz. Holding the box close to her, Meg realized her nervousness. With one hand she reached up and felt her hair. Meg turned and looked in the mirror. Quickly she pulled another curl over the place where the missing one had been. Too late she had a second thought about what she had done. "Will anyone notice?" she asked nervously.

Laura put an arm around Meg. "Molly will notice," she said. "And that's all that really matters now."

SOMEWHERE OVER
THE RAINBOW

Meg's eyes flew open. She suddenly sat up straight in her bed. Her breath came in quick gasps. Pushing her hair out of her face she looked up at the wall clock.

"Four-thirty-seven!" she said with relief. "Oh, thank goodness!" She fell back down on her pillow. A dream had awakened her. She was running to catch the plane to Kansas. As she weaved her way through the crowds, a businessman also in a hurry bumped against her and sent her precious 'N' Stuff box flying. The box opened and out fell everything the girls had so carefully selected to send to Molly. As the super-ball rolled away, Meg watched in amazement as the twin-hearts barrette came to life and floated away, too. Everything got caught in a whirlpool of wind and Meg could only stand watching helplessly as her cutoff curl bounced down the up escalator. It was a terrible dream and Meg was glad to be awake and out of it now.

She looked at the clock again. Still four-thirty-seven. A few more ticks and tocks and it would be four-thirty-eight, two hours and fifty-two minutes from the time her alarm was set to go off. Her plane was scheduled to leave at ten forty-five. It took almost an hour to get to the airport. Her parents wanted to allow plenty of time for traffic and checking Meg's suitcase. Meg couldn't believe she was this close to actually flying all that way alone. When she had first made the plans in her mind she only thought about the eight and a half inches on the map. Now she started thinking of the miles, and of being so far away from her friends and home. She'd spent the past week getting ready for this day. She'd packed and repacked, and she'd spent as much time as possible with Stevie and Laura. Everything seemed to be going so smoothly. But now at four-thirty-eight in the morning Meg was feeling scared.

She blinked her eyes in the darkness of her room. The streetlight outside her house made a streak of light on her wall and caught the clock in its beam. There was no way Meg could ignore the time with that light framing it. There was nothing for her to do now except lie in bed and think.

She tried to imagine what Molly's room would look like in Kansas. Probably exactly like her room here, Meg thought. That's certainly what she would do if she had to move. The seconds ticked away and Meg started blinking in time to the ticking. A minute of this was about all she could take. Suddenly she jumped out of bed, turned on her desk lamp, and pulled out a piece of her kitten stationery. Meg decided that at four-forty in the morning the perfect thing to do was to write a good-bye letter to Laura and Stevie. She thought for a minute and then began to write:

Dear Laura and Stevie,

It is four-forty-one in the morning and I'm wide awake. I can't believe that when you read this I'll be in the air and on my way to see Molly. I wish we could all go, but I will try my best to make sure Molly thinks of all of us. It will be great to be with her, but I will miss you both so much. I hope you think of me when you're riding in the Crispin Landing Fourth of July Parade. I'll be on my own for the very first time. This will be my most independent Independence Day! Write to me in Kansas. I'll write to you, too.

Best Friends 4-Ever,

Meg

Having finished her letter, Meg folded it up, put it in an envelope, and wrote both Stevie's and Laura's names on it. She put the letter on top of her bulging blue suitcase, which now stood by her door, ready to go. Meg's mother would have to deliver the letter for her so the girls would be able to read it while Meg was flying. Next to the suitcase was Meg's tote bag from her visit to the aquarium. Outlines of whales and porpoises swam happily on the turquoise-blue background. Inside the bag was the box for Molly.

At least my nightmare won't come true if I keep it in the tote bag! Meg thought as she flopped back into bed. It was still only a little after five o'clock in the morning. She could close her eyes and at least *try* to fall back asleep, even though she was sure that would be impossible. Meg lay there less than two minutes before she was asleep.

Brrrrrring! The alarm. Meg reached out a sleepy arm and turned off the rude awakener.

"Boy!" she said to Marmalade, who had come out from under the bed to investigate the noise. "Where did the time go?"

"Oh, good," her mother said, peeking in to check on Meg. "You're up. And you know what you're wearing on the plane?"

"My jean skirt and my red-and-white-checked blouse," Meg replied.

"That'll look nice. Come down when you're ready and eat a good breakfast. It's almost a four-hour plane ride from Providence to Kansas City." Mrs. Milano left Meg to finish dressing. It didn't take Meg long to shower, brush her hair and teeth, dress, and carry her tote bag and the letter downstairs. The suitcase would have to be left for her father. It weighed a ton by Meg's measurements.

The Milano family was finally loaded into the car and just about to pull out of the driveway when Meg called out, "Stop!" She had just buckled her seat belt and was adjusting her skirt when she looked out the rear window and saw Laura and Stevie racing down her street on their bikes. As they rode they carried something that Meg couldn't make out at first. They got a little closer and a big smile spread over Meg's face. Held between the two girls was a big banner tacked to two sticks. It said, FRIENDS 4-EVER — MOLLY, STEVIE, LAURA, AND MEG!

Meg undid her seat belt and got out of the car to get a better look at the beautiful thing the girls had made.

"Like it?" Stevie called out, as they pedaled by and turned around to pass by again.

"In your honor!" Laura added. They rode by one more time and then biked up to Meg and let the banner fold up on itself.

"You guys are incredible!" Meg laughed through tears of happiness, tiredness, and sadness at leaving Stevie and Laura.

"We couldn't let you miss the whole Fourth of July Parade," Stevie said. "At least you got to see our part of it."

"Thanks a lot," Meg said sincerely. As the three girls hugged and said their good-byes, Mr. Milano had to hurry them. Quickly, Meg grabbed the letter from the car and handed it over.

"I'm sorry, lambkins," he said to Meg, "but it's really time for us to go."

"Okay, Daddy," said Meg, breaking the hold on her friends. She climbed back into the car and strapped herself in again. As the car pulled slowly out of the driveway, all three girls yelled things at once.

"Don't forget to write!" said Meg.

"Say hello to Molly for us," said Laura.

"Don't do anything I wouldn't do," said Stevie.

They waved to each other until Meg's car was out of Stevie's and Laura's sight, and the bikes and banner were out of Meg's sight. Meg rode the rest of the way in a kind of tired silence. Her mother chattered cheerfully while her father sang, *"We're off to see the wizard,"* and Meg just closed her eyes and laid her head back. Going away was scary.

Mr. Milano had been right in hurrying her along. The time spent saying good-bye to Stevie and Laura did make them a little late. When they arrived at the airport, Mr. Milano dropped Meg and her mother off and went to park the car. Meg's mother checked the big blue suitcase and found the gate number where Meg's plane would be boarding. They hurried down the busy corridor, pushing past dozens of other rushed travelers, until they finally reached Gate 42. A flight attendant was waiting, holding up a sign with Meg's name on it.

"Passengers on Flight 425 to Kansas City International may begin boarding at Gate 42," a pleasant announcer's voice said.

The flight attendant came up to them. "Are you Meg?" she asked sweetly.

"Yes," answered Meg, nervously. "But I can't go yet. My father isn't here."

"You'll just have to go, Meg. He must have had trouble — " Mrs. Milano started to say.

"Meg!" Mr. Milano's voice called down the long hall. The tall figure of her father reached the gate just in time. Meg gave him a big hug, throwing her tote bag around his waist. "You couldn't leave without a hug from me, could you?" Her father laughed, hugging her back. "Now you have a good trip and most important, have a good time."

"Here's your name badge so the attendants on the plane will know you." The flight attendant smiled, pinning the badge on Meg's shirt. "Time to go on board."

"Oh," Meg stammered. "Well, all right. . . ." The crowd around her started moving and carried her with them along toward the ramp leading to the plane's door.

" 'Bye Mom," Meg called back excitedly. " 'Bye, Daddy!" She would have said more but didn't because of the flight attendant walking with her.

"Give our love to Molly," Mrs. Milano called

after Meg as she disappeared inside the huge airplane.

The noise of the terminal suddenly ceased as Meg walked inside the cabin of the plane. Another flight attendant greeted Meg by name and showed her to her seat by the window. Arrangements had been made ahead of time for Meg to receive special treatment, since she was a child traveling alone.

"If you need anything at all," the flight attendant said, "just push the button to call me." She pointed above Meg's head to a red call button.

"Thank you," Meg said in a small voice.

As the big red-cushioned seat folded around her comfortingly, Meg started to relax a little bit for the first time. There was an empty aisle seat next to her and she wondered if it would stay empty. It didn't. Down the aisle, heading for that seat, came the prettiest young woman Meg had ever seen. She looked like a model. The tall, slender girl was dressed in jeans, white cowboy boots with silver toe tips, a white shirt with pearl snap buttons, and a jean vest with white leather fringe on the back. Her waist-length black hair was pulled back in a sleek ponytail and held with a white leather tie. When she reached the seat next to Meg, she flashed a beautiful smile at her and threw her flat, black briefcase under the seat in front of hers.

"How y'all doin' today," said the woman to Meg in just about the friendliest voice Meg had ever heard.

"Uh, fine, I guess," Meg said, hesitating. "Are you a model?" she blurted out, unable to contain her curiosity about this striking girl.

"Yes, I am," replied the stranger as she sat next to Meg and tried to fit her long legs comfortably into the short space allowed them. "But for the next two weeks I'm not a model. I'm not anything. I'm just Becky Slade, hometown girl from Wichita, Kansas. And I'm on vacation starting right now!"

"You're from Kansas?" Meg gasped in disbelief. Her very worst fears all just came true. If this is what the Kansas kids were going to look like, something told her that her simple jean skirt and red-and-white-checked blouse were the absolute wrong choice. What would they think of her?

"Born and raised in Kansas," replied Becky proudly.

"Do you ride horses?" Meg asked worriedly, hoping the answer would be no.

"Sure I do," said Becky.

"I was afraid of that," mumbled Meg.

"And what are you going to be doing in Kansas? You're not from there, are you?" Becky said knowingly.

"Oh, you can tell? Well, no, I'm not from there," Meg said. Then she went on to tell Becky her whole story. She told her all about Molly and how the Friends 4-Ever Club got started. She told about the letters back and forth. She told about Stevie and Laura at home. She told about packing and the 'N' Stuff box.

" 'N' Stuff?" Becky asked curiously.

Meg took the box out of the tote bag, which rested under the seat in front of her. Becky admired the rainbow stickers Meg had put all over the box and appreciated all the special things inside. She didn't seem to think any of it was babyish or silly. And when Meg had closed up the box and put it away again, Becky told Meg a few stories of her own.

She too had a group of friends when she was Meg's age. They did everything together. They never ever thought they'd go separate ways, but the funny thing was they all did. Not one of them stayed in Wichita. Becky left to be a model after college. Another girl left to study to be a commercial airline pilot. Another got married right after college and moved to where her husband was going to graduate school. And another one left to study art history in Florence, Italy.

"Now," said Becky, "we all keep in touch when we can. Postcards mostly. And at holiday times we sometimes manage to all get home at the same time and see each other. We still consider ourselves 'friends forever,' too, no matter where we are or what we're doing."

"Oh," was all Meg said. She thought for a minute. "That's really good." Meg was glad to hear Becky's stories. She liked this model from Kansas. Their talk was interrupted by the flight attendant bringing lunch. Meg was suddenly starving. She and Becky ate ham on croissant sandwiches and drank orange juice together while Meg asked a million questions about what it was like to be a real model. She found out from Becky that modeling was fun, but it was also a lot of hard work.

When they'd finished their lunch and the trays were taken away, Becky took out her black case and showed Meg what was inside. It was full of beautiful photographs of Becky looking all different ways and wearing all different outfits. In one picture she had on a very fancy formal gown. Her hair was swept up on top of her head. She looked much older in the picture than she did in person. In another photo, Becky wore a pair of shorts with pink watermelon slices painted all over them. The top was one big watermelon slice. Her hair was down straight. In this picture she looked much younger than she did in person.

Now that Meg knew Becky, she could see that the pictures and the clothes didn't really tell what the real Becky was like. Or maybe, thought Meg, she's like all of these pictures.

Becky closed up the case when the pilot's voice came over the loudspeaker announcing that they were preparing for landing at Kansas City International. Within the next fifteen minutes the plane had landed softly and safely on the ground. When it came to a halt, everyone except Meg stood up and started getting their bags from above and below the seats. Meg clutched her tote bag tightly. Her nervous feelings were coming back. As her new friend stood up, Meg felt small and afraid. Becky saw the expression on Meg's face.

"Don't worry, Meg. The folks in Kansas don't bite." Becky smiled and gave Meg's shoulders a friendly squeeze.

Meg looked up into the model's face and said timidly, "I sure *hope* they don't."

MEG AND MOLLY

For weeks Meg had waited for this very moment. At last she was actually in Kansas. Really and truly in the state where Molly lived. And now that her plane had landed and she knew Molly and the Quindlen family were waiting for her on the other side of the airplane's door, Meg couldn't budge from her seat. Becky had already gotten off. The flight attendant asked Meg to wait for her to take her to her friends. Now the last passenger was just saying good-bye to the captain and co-pilot, and the flight attendant was coming down the aisle toward Meg.

I ♥ YOU

I

CHRIS
BOHAN

"Ready to go, young lady?" she asked with a smile.

"Oh! Yes, sure!" Meg said, jumping up and grabbing her tote bag.

"Are you nervous?" the woman asked after looking at Meg.

"Excited, I guess." Meg laughed. Then she thought, Excited. Maybe that really is what it is. She took a deep breath and tried to make the sick feeling in her stomach go away.

When she reached the door of the plane, the captain saluted her, smiled, and said, "Thanks for flying with us today, miss."

Meg was a little startled. "Oh, thank you," she said. One more step and she was out the door of the plane and walking through a narrow tunnel-like hall. It curved a little so she couldn't see the end of it. The flight attendant led the way confidently, and Meg had to hurry a little to keep up with her brisk steps. She switched the tote bag to the other hand and was adjusting the handles when she heard a familiar voice call out.

"Meg! Hey, Meg! Over here!"

Meg looked out into the crowd of unfamiliar faces and felt lost. She didn't see where the voice was coming from, although she knew *who* it was coming from. Her eyes darted from face to face, looking for one she knew.

"Meg!" came the voice from the crowd again. It was followed by a dog's excited barking. "Over here!" Meg turned in the direction of the voice and the bark and stared right at a girl who was smiling and screaming out her name. The girl held a dog Meg had seen many times. It was Riggs, the Quindlens' dog. But who was the girl holding him?

"Molly?" said Meg in disbelief. Instead of a short girl with long, dark hair, two missing front teeth, and choppy bangs that hung down over her eyebrows, the Molly that used to be, this Molly was tall. Her dark hair was cropped to just below her ears and it seemed to be mostly combed over to one side with no bangs at all. A straight, even, fully filled-in smile spread wide across this Molly's face. This Molly wore a jean jacket with leather fringe, cowboy boots, and a cowboy hat.

"Molly?" Meg said again, staring, wondering how in the world *her* Molly got so much taller and older-looking. Meg felt out of place in her silly jean skirt and too-neat checked blouse. The tote bag with the 'N' Stuff box in it suddenly weighed ten tons on her arm. She quickly wondered why she and Laura and Stevie had ever thought it might be a good idea to give Molly such a babyish thing as more 'N' Stuff.

"Yes!" shrieked Molly excitedly. "It's me! You look fabulous! You look great! Your hair is so long. I didn't know curly hair could get that long. It looks gorgeous!"

Molly was jumping up and down and Riggs was stretching out his pink, scratchy tongue trying to kiss Meg hello. Meg stood stock-still, in shock as she tried to adjust to how her friend looked and talked. Meg had never heard her use words like "fabulous" and "gorgeous" before. But now it was her turn to finally say something.

"Gosh. Molly. You look so . . . so fabulous!" Meg gave her friend and Riggs big hugs, which only lasted a second, because then Mrs. Quindlen was there ruffling up Meg's mass of blonde curls.

"Meg, honey!" Molly's mother said, hugging Meg. "It's wonderful to have you here. We're so excited that you could come! How was the flight?"

"How was the food?" Molly asked. "Was it

totally gross like all airplane food is supposed to be?"

"How are your folks?" asked Mr. Quindlen, as he started to relieve Meg of the tote bag. Meg held onto the bag more tightly.

"Oh, I can carry that," she said quickly. "It's not heavy at all." Then she tried to answer all the questions over the noise of Riggs barking happily in all the excitement of an old friend visiting.

"The flight was great. The food was great. And, Molly!" Meg said, suddenly remembering the best part of the flight. "I met a model! A real model. Her name is Becky and she lives in Kansas!"

As the Quindlens steered the girls toward the baggage claim area, Meg talked and talked about Becky and her pictures. She noticed that as long as she was talking she didn't feel so strange about how different Molly looked to her. At least Riggs was the same, she thought. Then she noticed something else.

"Molly!" she gasped, stopping dead in her tracks. "I can't believe you did it!"

"Did what?" Molly asked, bewildered.

Meg pointed to Molly's left ear, the only ear

that wasn't covered by her hair. "You pierced your ears!" Meg was horrified. The only other girl she knew their age who had pierced ears was Shana, the girl Laura was friendly with in the After-School Program. And Shana wasn't really their age. She was older, but still in their grade. Meg had always thought Shana's spiky hair and black bicycle pants and pierced ears were a bit much. Now her dear friend, one of her best friends, her wonderful, sweet Molly had pierced ears, too!

"Well," said Mrs. Quindlen, rolling her eyes. "I'm afraid things are a little different here than back home."

"All the girls have them," Molly said quickly. "But I'm not allowed to wear dangly earrings. Only studs."

"*Small* studs," Mr. Quindlen elaborated.

"Like these," Molly said, pulling back her hair to give Meg a better look at the tiny horse-shoe earrings that dotted her small earlobes.

"Oh, cute," said Meg, taking a closer look. She touched her hand to her own earlobe and wondered for a second how she might look with pierced ears. "On you it's cute," Meg said, canceling out thoughts of herself with pierced ears.

"I had it done a couple of months ago. I was saving it for a surprise. It didn't hurt." Molly bounced along excitedly, feeling happy to finally have one of her old friends here to see everything that had now become familiar to her.

They reached the baggage claim area and only one suitcase was going around and around the luggage carousel. "That's mine!" Meg shouted, pointing to the big, blue, bulging canvas case.

Mr. Quindlen grabbed the heavy bag and lifted it down. "Wow!" he exclaimed. "What did you bring us, Meg, our old house? This thing is heavy."

"That's because Stevie and Laura did the packing for me. Stevie just grabbed practically everything I own and threw it in." Meg had a second of sadness at her own mention of Stevie and Laura. Seeing how different Molly looked made her miss her other two friends.

"Did they see you off at the airport?" Molly asked.

"No, but they did come over to say good-bye and show me the Friends 4-Ever banner they made for the Fourth of July Parade. Your name is on it, too!" Meg told Molly all about the idea of riding bikes and holding the banner with all their names on it. Molly thought it all sounded great, but as they walked to the Quindlens' car she changed the subject. She was as anxious to tell Meg about what she had been doing as Meg was to tell her about what the rest of the Friends 4-Ever Club was doing.

"Meg," said Molly excitedly, "you won't believe it when you see me ride Kristy's horse. It's almost like having my own horse, since I ride the same one all of the time. His name is Chocolate and he's the most beautiful thing you've ever seen." They reached the car and all piled in. Molly didn't stop talking. "Even Scotty can ride now."

"Hey!" Meg said. "Where *is* Scotty?" In her excitement about seeing Molly she had forgotten all about Molly's little brother, Scotty.

"He stayed home with Grandpa. He didn't want to drive all the way to the airport. Too far," Molly explained. "But not too far for Riggs," she said, patting him.

"How far is it to Cross Plains?" asked Meg.

"About an hour and a half," Mrs. Quindlen answered. "But it will go quickly, since you girls have so much to talk about."

"Yeah," said Molly. "I haven't even begun to

tell you all about Kristy and the rest of the gang. They're so incredible. They all ride horses and they let me ride with them all the time. Kristy is so great. I can't wait until you meet her. You'll like her, I'm sure. And you'll love Chocolate," Molly exclaimed.

"I do love chocolate," joked Meg, but Molly didn't catch it. She was already onto the next subject: the rodeo.

"We're all going to the rodeo. You, too, Meg. We'll be riding in the opening ceremony and you'll be . . ."

Molly's voice trailed off in Meg's mind. She was picturing the rodeo and Kristy and the rest of the Kansas kids. She could just imagine how they'd all be taller than she was and they'd all be wearing jeans and cowboy boots and T-shirts with horses and names of ranches on them. And there she would be, wearing a pair of navy blue camp shorts, a babyish sleeveless blouse, and her pink jellies. The picture was enough to make her almost break out into a nervous sweat.

". . . don't you think so, Meg?" Molly was saying.

"Uh, what?" Meg asked, having been caught with her thoughts elsewhere.

"I said, we're going to have a fabulous time, don't you think?" Molly repeated.

"Oh. Yeah. We are," Meg stammered. "Yes! We're going to have an incredible time."

Mrs. Quindlen was right. The time did pass quickly. Molly talked and talked the whole hour and a half. Meg felt tired. She had woken up at four thirty-seven that morning, gained an hour with the time change from Rhode Island to Kansas, but now it was almost four o'clock in the afternoon, Kansas time. In the middle of one of Molly's sentences Meg's eyes just closed and the Quindlens let her sleep the rest of the way.

She missed the first sight of open prairie, vast fields of corn, and silo after silo. She woke up just as the car was slowing down to go over the railroad tracks that cut Cross Plains in half. The small, dusty town kind of grew up around the train tracks. Meg opened her sleepy eyes and saw a small restaurant called Annie's Cafe. Next to Annie's was a general store, then a dress shop, and then Quindlen's Hardware Store.

"Hey! There's your name!" shouted Meg in surprise.

"That's Grandpa's store," explained Molly. "That's where I met Kristy."

Kristy's name again. Meg couldn't help but notice that Molly talked about Kristy so much she didn't have breath left to ask too much about Laura and Stevie.

"Yeah," said Meg. "We know. Stevie and Laura and I read all about it in your letters." Meg hoped that by saying "we" it would make Molly talk about "them," meaning all of the Friends 4-Ever.

"Oh," gushed Molly. "I just wish you *all* could meet Kristy."

"Well, here we are!" Mr. Quindlen said cheerfully as he turned the car down a long dirt road. Meg could see down it. There was nothing but open prairie on either side. The green grasses were dotted with cornflowers and buttercups, making it a beautiful scene to see. At the end of the road stood an old farmhouse. Meg could see that the main house had been added onto in a lot of different places. Long, one-story additions stretched out from both sides of the two-story building.

"Wow!" said Meg, sitting up straighter in her seat to get a better look. "This is neat!" The house looked old, but it also looked interesting. "It's big," she said, somewhat surprised. She had never really imagined what Molly's new house would look like. When she thought of Molly she always thought of the small Cape Cod-style houses they all lived in, in Crispin Landing. It never crossed her mind that the house she moved to would be bigger and maybe even better.

"Come on up and I'll show you my room," Molly said excitedly, when her father had pulled the car right up in front of the house. Molly led the way and Meg followed, still carrying the tote bag. Riggs followed at their heels.

"You girls go ahead and I'll bring your bag in, Meg," Mr. Quindlen called after the already-gone girls.

"Hi, Grandpa!" Molly called as she went through the screen door that led to a big, old parlor. "Hi, Scotty!" No one answered. "They must be out for a walk," Molly explained. "Come on up." She headed up the stairs, two at a time. Riggs ran ahead and waited for them in Molly's room.

Meg tried to look all around as she followed Molly. She could see there were a lot of nooks and crannies that the Friends 4-Ever Club would love to turn into meeting places.

"Well, here it is," Molly said, leading Meg into a dark paneled room. "Like it?"

Meg was completely surprised. The dark wood walls were covered with posters of horses. The shelves were filled with plastic horses, china horses, and more pictures of horses. Hanging over the doorway was a horseshoe. On an old maple desk there were two pictures. One was of Meg, Stevie, and Laura dressed to look like Molly for Halloween. The other was of Molly dressed almost the way she was dressed today, standing next to a big chocolate-colored horse. On the other side of the horse was another girl who was even taller than Molly. Molly saw Meg looking at the picture.

"Oh!" she said happily. "That's Kristy. And that's Chocolate! Isn't he gorgeous?"

Meg sat down on one of the high, over-stuffed twin beds. As she looked around Molly's room, she wondered how Molly could stand such a dark room after having her bright, light room in Crispin Landing. Didn't she miss the wallpaper with the pink houses on it? Didn't she miss her white canopy bed? And since when did horse posters make better decorations than ballet posters? Meg was confused.

"My mom said I could fix it up any way I wanted," Molly explained to Meg as she helped her unpack. "Isn't it *so* great?"

The big suitcase was finally emptied. All that was left to unpack was the tote bag. Meg figured she might as well get that over with. Pulling out the sticker-covered box, she handed it to Molly. "This is from Laura and Stevie and me," she said, feeling a little silly. "It's new stuff for your 'N' Stuff box."

"Oh, great!" said Molly, taking the box. She opened it up without even mentioning all the special rainbow stickers on the outside. For the next minute she sat on the other over-stuffed bed and laid out the things in the box. "Cute," she said about the twin-hearts barrette.

"That's from Laura, to remind you our hearts are always with you," Meg said. Why did she feel so silly saying it now?

"Oh, neat!" said Molly, bouncing the super-ball Stevie had put in the box.

Meg didn't say anything. Then Molly picked up the curl. She could see right away that it came from Meg's mass of blonde hair. Suddenly Molly got tears in her eyes. It lasted only a second, then she stood up and gave Meg a big hug.

"Thanks, guys," Molly said to Meg. "You're really the best friends ever." Then, as quickly as the tears came, they went. "Hey, tomorrow is going to be a fabulous day!" she said, changing the subject. "Tomorrow I've planned it so you'll meet Kristy and all the rest of the kids. You're gonna love them."

"Molly?" Mrs. Quindlen interrupted with a call up the stairs. "Honey, if Meg is all settled, would you mind coming down now and setting the table?"

"I'll help," Meg said to Molly.

"Oh, no you don't," said Molly. "This is your first night here. Tonight I'll do it all. You can finish getting your stuff organized how you want it. I'll go down."

"Okay," said Meg, grateful for the chance to be alone with her thoughts for a little while.

"Coming, Mom!" Molly called, as she bounded down the stairs. Riggs didn't follow this time. Instead he came over to Meg and nuzzled against her.

"Well, I guess you miss your old friends, don't you, Riggs," whispered Meg. Now it was quiet in Molly's room. Meg sat still for a moment, scratching Riggs behind his ears. Looking around the room, Meg saw her stationery on the bed and decided to use the time to put her feelings down on paper. It was hard to understand how Molly was acting. Wasn't she at all upset about being stuck in Kansas with those kids? A letter to Laura and Stevie would help Meg understand her own feelings at this moment. The main feeling, she thought, was loneliness. She missed home, and that's how she began her letter.

Dear Laura and Stevie,

I'm here! So how come I wish I were there? I miss home and I miss you both. Right now I'm sitting in Molly's room alone (except for Riggs, who hasn't changed a bit). My suitcase is unpacked and Molly is downstairs helping her mother with dinner. The plane ride was fun. I met a real model and we talked the whole way.

Molly and her parents met me at the airport. *Her parents look exactly the same. Molly looks completely different. Are you ready for this? She has pierced ears!!! She looks older. I don't mean she has wrinkles or anything, but her hair is short and over to one side so you can see her earrings. She was so happy to see me, and I know it's a good thing I'm here. Tomorrow I will meet Kristy and the other Kansas kids. I hope they like me. Molly liked the 'N' Stuff, I guess. She seems really happy. Should we be happy about that? I guess I was sort of hoping she'd act a little sorry that she's not coming home. Oh, well, I'll write when I find out more. So far no tornadoes or flying houses. I miss you a lot.*

Friends 4-Ever and Ever,

Meg

Meg read her letter over. "So far no tornadoes," she read. She was referring to *The Wizard of Oz* and the tornado that swept Dorothy away. As she remembered the scene from the movie, a surprising thought hit Meg.

Maybe if I tap my shoes together three times and say, "There's no place like home," I could get back there. Meg could hardly believe her own thoughts. Now why would I want to get back home? she wondered. I just got here!

"Meg! Dinner!" Molly's voice called from downstairs.

"Here I come!" she called back. And here I am, she thought. In Kansas. With Molly. At last.

NIGHT AND DAY

Meg was so tired she practically fell into bed. Dinner had been fun and full of questions from the Quindlens about their old neighborhood and their old house. Meg filled them in on how nicely Mrs. Hansen had fixed up their house while she was renting it. She told them funny stories about the last days of school and horror stories about things Mrs. Higgle said and did to Laura's class.

As they all ate and talked, Meg noticed that it was Molly's parents who seemed most interested in home. Molly listened quietly and often changed the subject to the rodeo that was coming up, or Chocolate, or Kristy and the other kids. Now that it was finally bedtime, Meg was determined to keep her eyes open long enough to get Molly talking about something other than horses.

Before Meg had the chance to start the conversation, Molly called out to her in the dark from her bed. "Meg? Are you awake?"

"Uh-huh," answered Meg. "Are you?" They both laughed.

"I'm glad you're here," Molly said.

Good, Meg thought. Now she's going to talk about us, finally. "I'm glad I'm here, too," she said quietly back to Molly. "We all miss you so much."

"Yeah, me, too," Molly began. "I thought you'd never get here to meet Kristy and Tammy and the rest of the kids. Tomorrow's going to be a great day."

Meg was surprised. Instead of thinking about how great it was going to be for Kristy and Tammy and the rest of the kids to meet Meg, Molly only cared about *her* meeting *them!* Meg couldn't believe it. But she was just too tired to talk or think about it anymore. Against her will, Meg's eyes closed and didn't open again until morning.

Meg thought she had probably never seen anything brighter than the Kansas sun that was streaming through the calico-curtained window in Molly's room. Its brightness woke her from a deep sleep, and at first she couldn't place where she was. Then when her eye caught sight of the horseshoe hanging points-up over the doorway, she remembered. She looked over to Molly's bed and was surprised to see Molly wasn't in it and the bed was all made up. Meg jumped out of bed and rushed to get dressed.

Oh, no, she thought as she looked through her clothes. How do I know what to wear if I don't know what Molly's wearing? She decided a safe bet was jeans. When she went into the bathroom to wash, she found a surprise waiting for her. Neatly folded and sitting on the side of the sink was a T-shirt with a note pinned to it.

"Welcome to Kansas! Here's your first souvenir. Love, Molly."

Meg held up the shirt and saw a picture of a horse and the words "Cross Plains Rodeo

Round-up" across the front. It was red and would look perfect with her jeans. She put it on, fluffed up her curls, made her bed, and went downstairs to look for Molly.

"You look fabulous!" said Molly, who was just coming in from outside. "I just went out to pick some buttercups for the table. See if you like butter." Molly held the small bouquet under Meg's chin. The yellow flowers reflected yellow onto Meg's face. "Yup," said Molly. "You like butter. Your chin is yellow."

"And I love the shirt!" said Meg, happy to see that Molly, too, was wearing the same T-shirt, only in blue. Hers also looked perfect with her jeans. In fact, the two girls looked like they belonged together.

Meg felt a lot better today than she did yesterday. The breakfast table was already set, and there were plates of muffins, donuts, eggs, bacon, and waffles. Scotty, Grandpa, and Mr. Quindlen all came in together from outside. Scotty was very excited about something.

"And, Grandpa, did you see how that gopher ran when he heard us singing?" Scotty was almost six years old. He had straight dark hair and big blue eyes. When he talked excitedly his eyes brightened and his hair fell down almost into them.

"Those gophers really *go fer* our singing, don't they Scotty?" Grandpa joked as he pulled out his chair and sat down. " 'Morning, girls," he said to Meg and Molly. "You two are up bright and early. Got big plans today?"

"I'll say," said Molly. "I'm taking Meg over to Kristy's and we're going to see Chocolate and the other horses."

"You'll be careful, won't you Molly," said Mrs. Quindlen, carrying in a pitcher of syrup for the waffles. "Meg's never ridden a horse before."

That reminded Meg of her feelings the night before. She didn't want to spoil the day, so she tried to shake them off. In fact, though, now that Mrs. Quindlen mentioned riding, Meg admitted to herself that she was very afraid of falling off the horse.

"I probably won't ride, Mrs. Quindlen," she said. "I'll just watch."

"Never say never," Molly said cheerfully, shoving a last bit of waffle into her mouth. "Ready?"

Meg took one more bite of her food and

washed it down with a last slurp of juice. "As ready as I'll ever be, I guess," she said.

"I'll call Kristy and tell her we're on our way," Molly said, heading for the phone in the kitchen.

Meg heard her dial. Then she heard, "Kristy? Hi. Molly. Meg's here and we'll be at your house in a flash. Okay? Okay. See ya. 'Bye." She hung up.

Meg felt strange. Even though Molly had talked about Kristy and written letters about her, hearing her actually talking *to* Kristy was different. And now, instead of feeling like the *old* friend, for some reason Meg felt like she was the *new* friend.

"Hey, Meg? You coming?" Molly said, holding the door open.

Molly seemed to have no idea about how Meg was feeling and Meg was glad. She had always shared all her thoughts with Molly before, but right now Meg wasn't ready to. Instead, Meg put on her biggest smile, and followed Molly out the door. The two girls sang "Follow the Yellow Brick Road" all the way to Kristy's house. After about a ten-minute walk, Meg could see the silhouette of a house against the bright blue sky.

As they got closer to the house, Meg could also see the outlines of three horses and one person.

"There's Kristy," Molly said happily. "And she's got the horses all ready for us!"

"Well," said Meg. "I guess it looks like I'll be riding after all."

"No you won't," said Molly. "You'll be riding Starry Night. There is no horse named After All!" Both girls laughed at Molly's joke. They were still laughing when they reached the slim girl holding the reigns of three very big horses.

"Kristy!" Molly shouted. "And Chocolate!" Molly went right up to the sleek chocolate-brown animal. Even though Molly looked taller to Meg at the airport, next to the horse she looked pretty small. Chocolate greeted Molly with a nuzzle and a lick.

Molly giggled. "See how gentle he is, Meg?"

"So this is Meg," said Kristy with a crooked-toothed smile. "Hey, Meg."

Meg noticed right away that Kristy had pierced ears, too. Her long sun-streaked hair waved gently down her back and allowed Meg to see the small gold hoops in her ears. Kristy was tall, too, and her flat, beat-up loafers didn't add an inch to her height. She wore faded jeans, a plain white T-shirt, and tied to one of her belt loops was a red bandanna. Freckles dotted her tanned face, but even freckles didn't make her look as young as Meg felt standing next to her.

"Molly's told me a lot about you," Meg said politely.

"And some of it was good." Kristy laughed, making a joke on herself.

For half a second Meg felt like she was talking to Stevie. That was just the kind of thing Stevie would have said. Meg laughed in spite of her feelings.

"She's told me a lot about you, too," Kristy went on, "and Laura and Stevie and the Friends 4-Ever and Crispin Landing and — "

"All right, all right." Molly giggled. "So maybe I did talk about them too much."

"Just kidding, Mol," said Kristy.

Then Meg got another strange feeling. Molly had spent the whole night talking about Kristy and the Kansas kids. Now she realized they had all heard about the Crispin Landing kids, too. She was just cheering up when the sound of approaching horses made the three horses Kristy was holding start to get restless. Three riders were coming toward them.

The Terrible Three! Meg thought to herself. As soon as she saw the three girls on horseback, Meg was sure they were the ones Molly had written about months before — the ones who had been so mean to her when she first moved there.

The Terrible Three slowed their horses down, climbed off, and walked them the rest of the way. Meg felt a little shy as the three girls in jeans came closer. They all walked with the same long stride. And they were all looking at Meg.

"Hey!" said Kristy, cheerfully. "You're just in time to meet Meg."

"So, Crispin Landing comes to Cross Plains . . . again," said the girl with the short red hair.

At least *she's* the same height as I am, Meg thought.

"Tammy," said Molly to the red-haired girl, "this is my friend Meg."

"Friends 4-Ever, right?" said the plumper girl standing next to Tammy. "Hi, I'm Maddie." Maddie steadied her black-and-white-spotted horse as she spoke.

"And I'm Claire," said the third girl, patting her own dark brown horse.

"Hi," said Meg. "Nice horses."

"Yeah," said Kristy. "So let's ride 'em!"

All the girls easily got up into the saddles. From high up on Chocolate, Molly tried to direct Meg and help her climb onto the big black mare with a white star on her forehead.

"Don't worry, Meg. Starry Night is just about the gentlest horse in the stable."

"Maybe you'd rather ride Nightmare." Tammy laughed. "She's exactly what her name says."

"No thanks," Meg said, struggling to get her sneakered foot into the stirrup. Holding the horn on the Western-style saddle, Meg pulled herself up and swung one leg over. "This one seems fine to me." She patted Starry Night's mane.

Meg looked down and realized that the ground was a long way away. Starry Night sensed Meg's nervousness and pranced a little bit. Meg shrieked. Before the other girls could stop her, Meg's horse took off at a brisk gallop. Holding on as tightly as she could, Meg closed her eyes and let the wind cool her hot face. Without control, Meg bounced up and down in the saddle until she could feel each bite of breakfast banging against the sides of her stomach.

"Hold on, Meg!" Molly called out.

"Ride 'em!" yelled out Tammy.

While Kristy and Molly rode after Meg, the other three sat atop their horses and cheered Meg on. Meg couldn't hear anything except her own screams. And then just as suddenly as she had started running away, Starry Night slowed down and started walking in a gentle, even gait. Meg stopped screaming, but her hands still gripped the saddle and reigns so tightly her knuckles were white. Her feelings of terror were replaced by a surprising calm as she realized she had just ridden a runaway horse and not fallen off!

"Are you all right, Meg?" Molly shouted, as she and Kristy caught up with the runaways.

"Wow!" said Kristy, moving her horse alongside Meg's. "And you're the one who never rode a horse before! You were great!"

Now that it was over, Meg burst into tears. All her fear came out in big teardrops, and she couldn't stop herself from crying. Molly got down off Chocolate and helped Meg climb down, too. Kristy took the reigns of the two riderless animals and led them home.

"I guess we'd better go back to my house," Molly said to Kristy.

"I'm sorry," cried Meg, feeling terrible about ruining the whole day.

"I'm just glad you're all right," Molly said, putting a comforting arm around her friend.

The other three girls were waiting as Meg and Molly walked behind Kristy and the horses. "Nice riding, Meg," Maddie said.

"You'll be ready for the rodeo for sure!" Tammy joked.

"Don't," said Claire. "She's crying."

"We'll see you tomorrow," said Molly to the girls. Meg just kept her head down, hoping the others wouldn't see just how much she'd been crying.

" 'Bye," said Meg. "See you."

On the way home Molly tried to make Meg feel better. "You were incredible," she said. "You didn't even fall off. When I first rode Chocolate I fell off three times and he wasn't even running!"

"You did?" Meg asked, brightening a little.

"Well, maybe it was only two times, but anyway, you didn't fall off at all. I'm sure Tammy and Maddie and Claire think you're incredible, too."

Meg wasn't so sure about that, but she did feel better by the time they reached Molly's house. All the Quindlens worried and fussed over her when they heard about the runaway horse. But that night while Molly took a shower, Meg got out her stationery and wrote her real feelings in a letter to Laura.

Dear Laura,

Since I just wrote you last night, you might think I don't have much to say. But I do. If you were here I'd call an emergency club meeting. It really is an emergency this time. I'm homesick. I miss you, I miss Stevie, I miss Crispin Landing, I even miss Marmalade. I'd rather have a cat than a horse any day.

Today I rode a giant horse named Starry Night. I was so scared. She ran away with me on her back. I didn't fall off, but it might have been better if I had. Then at least there would have been a good reason for me to cry, which I did . . . a lot! Right in front of all of Molly's Kansas friends. They just watched me, and I felt like such a baby.

I liked Molly's friend Kristy, but I didn't really like The Terrible Three. I only met them for a few minutes, but being with them made me feel funny. Inside I felt like an outsider.

There is going to be a rodeo on my last day here and I think Molly wants me to be in it with her and her friends. The only thing I want to be in is the Crispin Landing Fourth of July Parade, but I guess I won't be doing that this year.

I wish I could talk to you so you could help me figure out what to do. I know Molly will want me to try to ride the horse again and see her friends more. Yeccch. The only friends I want to see are you and Stevie. And the absolute only thing I ever want to ride is my bike.

Write to me please. Maybe Stevie was right. Maybe she should have been the one

*to come here instead of me. I promise I'll try
not to let you down. You can still count on
me, but it just won't be as easy as I thought.*

Friends 4-Ever and Ever,

Meg

When she finished writing, Meg folded the letter up and put it in the envelope with the letter she had written the night before. She tucked the letter into the tote bag. She didn't want Molly to see it. But the funny thing was that Meg wasn't the only one to write a letter.

After Molly took her shower, it was Meg's turn in the bathroom. That's when Molly took out her stationery and wrote a letter of her own. She kept the paper covered in case Meg finished her shower quickly. In fact, she was only able to write half a page before Meg was done. Not wanting Meg to see the letter, which began "Dear Stevie," Molly quickly stuffed it under the desk blotter and played with Riggs.

"Well, at least you have Riggs here to remind you of some of the fun times we all had at home," Meg began.

Molly gave the dog a last scratch and hopped into her bed. Again, she changed the subject from home to Kansas. "Riggs even has friends here." Molly smiled. "He's really happy, aren't you, Riggs?"

Meg was disappointed. So far there was just no getting through to Molly. "Well, good-night, Molly," she said with a yawn.

"See you in the morning," Molly answered, turning out the light. In a few minutes everyone was sound asleep, even Riggs.

BLINK AND YOU'LL MISS IT

That first day in Cross Plains would always be "the crying day" in Meg's mind. She was sure she'd never get over the embarrassment of having Kristy and the other girls see her screaming and crying as her horse whisked Meg away from them. Her plan had been to come to Kansas to show Molly that old friends are the best friends. Instead, what she'd shown her was that old friends are the babyish friends. No matter what else happened, Meg promised herself she would not cry. However, she almost cried tears of joy when Mrs. Quindlen announced there would be no more horseback riding until some lessons could be arranged for Meg.

Molly didn't even seem to mind not seeing Chocolate for a few days. "There are plenty of other things to do," she said. "I've been making plans ever since I found out you were coming."

The two girls spent one day picking wild flowers and making beautiful wreaths for their hair. They spent another day looking through the treasures in Molly's Grandpa's old attic. And the day after that they explored the rest of the house and basement looking for things from the "old days" when Grandpa and Grandma first built the old house. Grandma had died and now Grandpa was not well, but through the years they had collected trunks full of interesting memories that Meg and Molly loved getting lost in.

These were the kind of days Meg had hoped for. She liked having Molly all to herself. In fact, she had almost forgotten what she had written in her letters to Stevie and Laura until the mail brought a letter back from Laura. As usual, Laura's letter was good and long. What was not usual was the advice that Laura gave in her letter.

Dear Meg,

    I can't believe I'm giving you advice since you're usually the one to give advice to me. But your letters sound like you need some help. You don't sound like the same Meg that left here. I think maybe you forgot why you went to visit Molly. You wanted to see her to remind her of who her best best friends are. But, Meg, I think Molly already knows who her best best friends are. She didn't want to move away from us. She had to. You say you are feeling homesick after only one day. Just think how Molly must feel being away from home for almost a whole year! If we are really her best, best friends we should be happy that she has some new friends to make her feel less homesick.

    Maybe you aren't seeing the Kansas kids the way Molly sees them. Just because they act different doesn't mean they aren't nice.

I think that while you are there you should try to see them as Molly's friends and try to fit in with them. I know Kansas will never be Crispin Landing. But Molly will always be Molly. And we'll all always be . . .

Friends 4-Ever

Laura

When Meg finished reading Laura's letter, her first feeling was anger. She was a long way from home, feeling homesick and out of place with a bunch of kids she didn't even know. Instead of feeling sorry for Meg, it sounded as if Laura was on the side of the Kansas kids. What could she mean by "maybe you aren't seeing the Kansas kids the way Molly sees them"?

Just as Meg was putting the letter away in her tote bag, Molly came up the stairs and into the room. "Today," she announced in an official-sounding voice, "we have on the agenda a good, old-fashioned picnic."

Meg was glad to hear it. "Great," she said. "We can pack some sandwiches and look for things for our 'N' Stuff boxes. I need some Kansas souvenirs."

Quickly they packed the sandwiches, along with fruit, a thermos of lemonade, chips, and some homemade chocolate chip cookies. As Meg and Molly ran happily to what Molly called "her perfect picnic spot," Meg felt good. Now this is really the way it was supposed to be, she thought. Molly and me together again, just the way it used to be.

Her thoughts were interrupted by the sounds of giggles and voices. Already spread out in "her perfect picnic spot" were four blankets. There in a row were Tammy, Maddie, Claire, and Kristy, with their horses tied to trees behind them. Meg's heart sank.

"What took you so long?" shouted Tammy.

"We've been here for half an hour already," Maddie added.

"Better late than never," Claire said.

"Put your stuff down here," Kristy said, pointing to a spot next to her blanket.

As Meg tried to hide her souvenir-collecting bag, Molly ran right over to the horses and started feeding them some of the fruit from her lunch. The "perfect picnic spot" turned into the perfect spot for talking about horses, horses, horses, and Meg could only listen. What started out to be a great day turned into a just so-so day, and Meg was happy that night to have one more day of her stay over with.

The next day was not much better. The girls woke up early, ate a good breakfast, and then piled into Mr. Quindlen's car.

"Ready for a tour of exciting Cross Plains, Kansas?" Mr. Quindlen laughed as he headed the car toward town.

"We're going to the hardware store!" Molly said. "Now you'll get to see all the things I've been writing to you about all year."

Meg had a good picture in her mind of what the store looked like. Molly had written many letters describing the big books of wallpaper that she spent hours looking through. It was in one of these books that Molly had found her Crispin Landing room wallpaper. She and Meg and Stevie and Laura had spent many hours making up stories about the pink houses on that wallpaper. Thinking back on those times made Meg have a teary-eyed moment. She pressed her lips together hard so she wouldn't ruin this day with crying, too.

Her thoughts switched to other things about the store. Molly had given very detailed descriptions of all the brooms, tools, farm supplies, barrels of nails, hooks, ropes, cans of paint and varnish, and practically anything anyone might need to fix everything. Then Meg remembered one other thing Molly had liked so much about the store. The hardware store was where everyone in town met everyone else. Meg knew what that meant.

"There it is!" exclaimed Molly as the car drove up the main street of Cross Plains. Once again, Meg saw Annie's Cafe, and the dress shop, and the big sign that said QUINDLEN'S HARDWARE STORE. Mr. Quindlen pulled into the dirt driveway next to the store.

"Everybody out!" he said.

"*We* get to go in the back door," said Molly proudly, following her father and leading Meg into a small room that led into a larger storage room. They walked past piles of bagged concrete, rows of tall ladders, and sacks of grain, through a wide doorway into the main store. Meg looked around and saw exactly what she had imagined. Ceiling fans cooled the air and made the wrapped things on the shelves rustle

100

in their breeze. Meg liked the way her footsteps sounded as they made a light thud on the wide-planked wood floor.

Molly headed right around the other side of the big wooden counter. "Come around back here," she said to Meg. "You get to see the cash register and everything."

"Wow," said Meg, looking at the big, old-fashioned black cash register. "This thing is neat."

"It's as old as the store," said Molly. "Grandpa got it when he first joined his father at the store way back when." Molly started to show Meg all the yardsticks and grain scales and other store-keeper's things behind the counter when a boy's voice interrupted.

"Hey, Molly!" said a very tall, thin boy with hair the color of straw falling down over his forehead. "Ready for the rodeo?"

"Oh, hi, Jake," Molly said with a smile. "Meg, this is my friend Jake Landon. Jake, this is my friend Meg Milano."

"Hi, Meg," Jake said, smiling, too.

Meg suddenly became shy. She was also very surprised. Molly had never mentioned that *she* had any friends who were boys. None of them had any real friends who were boys, not since they were in nursery school. Now, here was Molly Quindlen, acting ordinary as could be, introducing her friend Jake Landon.

"Hi," said Meg timidly.

"How long are you staying?" Jake asked, pushing his hair off his forehead.

"Just about one more week. I've already been here for almost a week."

"Have you met all the kids?" Jake asked.

"She's met Kristy, Tammy, Claire, and Maddie," answered Molly for her. "And now she's met you. Where's Wayne?"

Wayne? Meg wondered. *Another* boy? She didn't know why she felt so surprised by Molly's having friends who were boys. It was no big deal, she guessed. But it was different from the way it was in Crispin Landing. There it seemed the girls stuck together and the boys stayed separate, except to bother the girls at recess or chase them on their bikes.

"He's riding," Jake said, explaining why Wayne wasn't with him, as he almost always was.

"Hi, guys!" Kristy poked her head in the front doorway. "I can't stop now. I have to get some things down the street. I'll see you later, though."

That was how the day at the hardware store went. Friendly faces popped in and out of the store all day long. Molly seemed to know everyone and Meg could almost see why Molly didn't absolutely hate living there. No sooner did Meg have that kindly thought than Tammy came into the store and changed Meg's mind. Dressed in dusty jeans and riding boots, the red-haired girl strutted saucily into the store. Her boots made loud thumps on the floor as she headed toward Meg, carrying something Meg recognized as belonging to her. With a kind of smirk on her face, Tammy held out a bag that Meg had decorated with stickers.

"This is yours, isn't it?" Tammy said, almost in an accusing voice. "I looked through it and found all this weird stuff, so I figured it must belong to you."

Tammy held the souvenir-collecting bag Meg had brought to the picnic the day before. She had collected a few things on the way to the picnic spot. At the time it had seemed worthwhile to pick up the old seed pod; the rock that glittered like gold in the sunlight; a feather from a high-flying chicken hawk; and a small bouquet of buttercups, which were now limp and melted-looking. But now, as Tammy held out these things to Meg, looking at the souvenirs as though they were a collection of poisonous snakes, Meg felt ridiculous.

"You left it at the picnic spot yesterday. I thought you might need it." Tammy laughed a little as she said this.

"Thank you," Meg said coldly, accepting the bag from the girl.

"That was so nice of you to bring it to her, Tammy," Molly said.

Meg was furious. Molly didn't even seem to notice the look on Tammy's face as she handed over the stuff. The tall girl didn't stay long. She said something about having to go finish her chores around the farm before dinner and left.

That night at the dinner table Mr. Quindlen talked about what a help the girls had been at the store that day. He told Mrs. Quindlen that they'd seen lots of Molly's friends and Meg had really gotten a feel for Cross Plains.

"Did you see the town then?" Molly's mother asked Meg.

"Well, we ate lunch at Annie's Cafe and walked up one side of Main Street and down the other side," Meg answered.

"That's why they say 'Cross Plains, blink and you'll miss it,' " Molly's grandfather said. "It's that small. But it's worth taking the second to see it. Some big things have happened in this small town. You can't always tell about a town just by looking at it."

Meg thought of Laura's letter again. Maybe that's what Laura meant, too, she thought. Maybe I've been blinking too much when I look at the Kansas kids. Then she remembered that look on Tammy's face and had another thought. Or maybe I should have blinked more and missed *her* completely!

"I have wonderful news for you girls," Mrs. Quindlen said as she passed Meg a platter of chicken. "While you all were busy in town I was busy lining up riding lessons for Meg!"

"Fabulous!" Molly shrieked excitedly. "Who's teaching her?"

"Your friend Tammy Travers," Mrs. Quindlen replied.

"What?!" Meg gasped. "Tammy?"

"She's perfect," said Molly. "She's the best

rider around. She even taught me. She'll have you ready for the rodeo just in time. When does she start?" Molly asked her mother.

"Tomorrow's the big day!" Mrs. Quindlen answered, looking at Meg.

Meg swallowed the bite of chicken she'd taken before Tammy's name had been mentioned. Mrs. Quindlen looked so pleased with what she had done that Meg didn't dare say anything more than, "Thanks. Thanks a lot." Later that night she did say more, a lot more.

Dear Laura and Stevie,

This time I need help from both of you. Tomorrow I start riding lessons. And the one who is teaching me is the worst of The Terrible Three. Her name is Tammy and I can tell already that she doesn't like me.

Today Molly and I went to her grandfather's hardware store. The first thing I found out is that Molly has more than just new girl friends. She also has boy friends! Not exactly boyfriends, but I mean friends who are boys!!! They all go riding together and they're all planning to be in this big rodeo. That's all anybody talks about around here. But back to Tammy.

She came into the store today to bring me something I left at the picnic we went on yesterday. I had collected some great nature souvenirs to bring home to show you. When Tammy handed the bag to me she called the stuff "weird" and said she knew it must be mine, like maybe I was weird. And now Mrs. Quindlen has arranged for Tammy to get me ready for the rodeo. What a mess. Where are you guys when I need you? Home, of course. And that's where I belong, too. Write soon. Write NOW! Help!

Your desperate Friend 4-Ever,

Meg

SUNNY DAYS AND STARRY NIGHT

"Meg? Meg?" Molly whispered her friend's name, trying to be gentle when waking her up. "Meg?" she said again, louder this time.

"Hmmmm . . ." moaned Meg, sleepily. She opened her eyes and saw Molly leaning over her, already dressed. "What time is it?" Meg asked.

"Six-thirty. We have to be over at Tammy's in half an hour, so you have to get up, okay?" Molly already had clothes out for Meg. She had laid out a pair of jeans, Meg's Camp Mohawk sweatshirt, and socks and sneakers.

"Oh, thanks," Meg said when she saw the

clothes. "Is that what I should wear for the lessons?"

"Yeah, it will be chilly so early, but Tammy wants to do it at this time so she can do her own practicing the rest of the day. She'll be riding in a lot of different events in the rodeo. We'll just ride in the opening ceremony."

"Oh, Molly, do you really think I'll be ready in just a week? I sure don't want to end up crying in front of the whole state of Kansas!" Even Meg had to laugh at the picture of her horse running away with her at a rodeo. "I'd probably be better off sticking to bike riding."

"Meg Milano," Molly scolded, "you're not going home until you can ride a horse, and that's that! Don't worry about a thing. Tammy is going to know exactly what to do with you."

"That's what I'm afraid of," Meg said. "What exactly will she do with me?"

"Nothing, if you don't get up and get ready. Hurry. I'll meet you downstairs." Molly gave Meg one more little nudge and then turned and left the room.

Meg got up quickly, got dressed, and joined Molly downstairs. She could hear Riggs barking outside. He was after something, as usual. Meg looked out Molly's window and saw the little dog running after some birds that had tried to grab a quick bite of seed before Riggs reached them. Seeing the birds eating made Meg hungry, too. She hurried downstairs and joined Molly for a quick breakfast. As the two girls headed out the door, Riggs came bounding up to them.

"No, Riggs," Molly said firmly. "You can't come with us. You'll chase the horses. Get inside." She led the yipping dog back into the house and shut the door. Then she and Meg turned down the road to Tammy's house. It was in the opposite direction from Kristy's and seemed like a long walk to Meg. It sure wasn't like Crispin Landing, where all the houses were close enough that you could see who was home and who wasn't before you walked all the way there.

"Isn't it great to walk so early in the morning?" Molly said, picking up the pace a little. "It's so quiet, except for the birds."

"It is pretty here," Meg agreed. "You really like it a lot, don't you?"

"At first I hated it," Molly began. "I was so busy missing you and Laura and Stevie that I didn't even want to give it a chance. I even felt mad at Grandpa for getting sick and making us have to move out here. But after a while I started getting used to things. It's different from home. But different isn't always terrible.''

"No, not always, I guess," Meg said thoughtfully.

"There's Tammy's house," Molly said, pointing. "And it looks like she's ready for you." In front of an old farmhouse there was a closed-in area. A circle of white clapboard fencing made a perfect riding ring, and Tammy was already sitting in the saddle on her horse. Next to her, Starry Night waited for Meg to try her luck one more time.

"Hi, Molly," Tammy said. "Oh, hi, Meg," she added reluctantly. "You forgot knee pads, elbow pads, and a helmet," Tammy said sarcastically. "In case you can't stay on, I mean."

Meg didn't know how to react. Was Tammy kidding? Molly laughed. "Oh, Tammy," she said, "Meg's not gonna fall off. Not with you teaching her."

"I got Starry Night for her," Tammy said to Molly, ignoring Meg completely. "Since she handled her so well the first time, I thought she might as well stick with her."

Now Meg knew Tammy must be kidding. She didn't exactly see having a horse run away with her as "handling" the horse. Meg felt a little afraid of Tammy. She turned to Starry Night and started to walk up to her cautiously.

"I'll wait over here," said Molly, going to lean up against a big tree.

"Good idea," Tammy said. "Leave her to me."

Please, *don't* leave me to this terrible girl, Meg thought. But Molly didn't seem to see anything strange about Tammy's behavior at all.

"Here," said Tammy, passing a carrot to Meg. Meg thanked her and started to take a bite. "Not you, silly. Give it to your horse."

Meg was embarrassed and nervous as she held the carrot out to Starry Night. The horse nibbled it while Meg held it.

"Hold your hand out flat," Tammy instructed. "Then she can't bite you."

Meg did as she was told. Starry Night finished the carrot and then licked Meg's palm. Meg laughed. "It tickles!" she giggled.

"Climb up," said Tammy in a no-nonsense voice. "The lesson is about to begin. And pay attention. I'm only doing this because Mrs. Quindlen asked."

Meg was ready to quit right then and there, she was so mad at Tammy. "Look," she said, getting up the nerve to tell Tammy what she thought, "I don't like this any better than you do, but I'm doing it for Molly."

"Well, so am I," said Tammy, annoyed. "I'm doing it because she's my friend."

"Well, she's my friend, too," Meg hissed, trying not to excite Starry Night.

All the while this was going on, Molly stood under the tree, watching and smiling, not able to hear what the girls were saying. As far as she could tell, the lesson was going well. Tammy had gotten Meg up on the horse and was leading her around the ring. After about half an hour, Molly walked over to the fence just in time to hear Tammy saying, "Will you be back tomorrow?"

"I wouldn't miss it," said Meg in a controlled voice. She swung her leg down off Starry Night and handed the reigns over to Tammy.

"I knew you could get Meg riding fast," Molly bubbled. "You're the perfect teacher. Thanks a lot, Tammy."

Meg never said a word to Molly about what had happened between her and Tammy. For some reason Meg felt like she would be tattling on the girl if she told. All the argument did, though, was make Meg even more determined to learn to ride. They went back the next day for a second lesson. Things were a little better, but not much. On the third day, though, something happened to change things.

Tammy began the lesson with the basics, as usual. "Hold your knees tightly against her sides," she said. "Pull gently on the right reign. Talk to her quietly. Let her get to know your voice. Let her see that you trust her."

Trust her? Meg thought, feeling too far off the ground and too nervous to talk at all. But Meg followed Tammy's directions and tried her hardest not to make any mistakes. Slowly but surely she began to feel almost comfortable, almost relaxed, and almost a little bit confident. She thought maybe even Tammy was noticing that she wasn't acting like such a total baby. Just as a small smile started to appear on her lips, a large bee came buzzing by and flew right onto Meg's forehead.

"Ouch!" Meg cried out, reaching a hand up to touch the spot where the bee had stung her. Immediately a large red welt appeared in the place where the bee's stinger was still stuck.

Molly came running over, and even Tammy walked her horse back to where Meg and Starry Night stood.

"Are you all right?" Tammy asked.

"What happened?" Molly asked worriedly.

Meg shook her head, still holding the spot. "I guess I'm all right," she said, holding back the tears. Then she moved her hand aside and the two girls saw the bee sting. "Well," said Tammy. "I guess the lesson's over for today."

"No," insisted Meg bravely. "I can still do more."

"Well, I can't," said Tammy. "It's time for me to stop anyway. But you did all right. I have to finish my morning chores and get Starry Night back to Kristy's before we practice for the rodeo. I'll see you tomorrow, same time."

Meg climbed down off Starry Night and handed her over to Tammy. The bee sting was still swelling, but Meg managed a smile and a "Thanks, Tammy." She couldn't believe her bad luck. Just when things had been going so well that stupid bee had to ruin things. Meg was so mad she hardly felt the sting anymore.

"You were great, Meg," said Molly. "Are you really all right?"

"Yeah, I guess so," Meg said. "It seems like horses and I just don't mix, that's all."

"It was a bee that stung you, not a horse!" Molly laughed. Meg laughed with her. When they got back to Molly's house a little ice brought down the swelling. The mail had come, and there was a letter to Molly and Meg from Stevie. The two girls read it together.

Dear Molly and Meg,

How are things in Kansas? You missed a great Fourth of July Parade. Laura and I were the stars of the whole thing with our Friends 4-Ever banner. We did bicycle tricks (well, I did the tricks and Laura did bicycle ballet). Now everyone in Crispin Landing knows that Stevie, Laura, Molly, and Meg are the best, best friends ever. Too bad we couldn't all be together for the parade. The rodeo sounds like it's going to be pretty neat, too. I wish we could see you two riding in it. I can't believe Meg is going to get on a horse. That's almost as brave as cutting off your curl, Meg! Gotta go! Laura's coming over for an emergency club meeting.

Yours 'til the hat band plays,

STEVIE

"Emergency club meeting!" said Meg, amazed. "Without me there to call it? I don't believe it!"

"I wonder what the emergency could be?" Molly said, frowning.

"Well, whatever it is, I guess it doesn't have anything to do with us," said Meg, trying to put it out of her mind so she wouldn't be so curious.

Mrs. Quindlen interrupted the girls to ask Molly to come downstairs and brush the burrs out of Riggs' fur. Molly tossed the letter to Meg on her way out and asked Meg to put it in her desk drawer.

"I'll be back in a flash," said Molly, grabbing a brush for Riggs.

Meg took the letter, folded it, and opened the drawer in the desk. She was about to lay the letter down when something caught her eye. It was a piece of Molly's rainbow stationery, and right away Meg could see that it was a half-written letter to Stevie. Meg knew she probably shouldn't read it, but there *it* was and Molly wasn't, and after all, they *were* a club. At least that's the excuse she gave herself as she began to read.

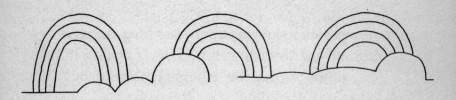

Dear Stevie,

Meg is in the shower and I don't have much time to write, but I just have to talk to you. It's really great having Meg here, but it really makes me feel terrible. I thought I would feel so happy to see someone from home, but instead, all it is doing is making me miss home and my real friends more than anything. All Meg talks about is you and Laura and the club. She keeps telling me about things in Crispin Landing and about all the things you're doing without me. Every

time she starts to talk I have to change the
subject so I don't start crying. I just wish

That's where the letter stopped. Meg's eyes were wide. Then she heard Molly coming and started to put the letter back. Instead, she stood holding it when Molly came into the room.

"What's wrong?" said Molly, seeing Meg's expression. Then she saw the letter. "Oh. You found my — "

"I'm sorry, Molly. I know I shouldn't have read it. But I'm glad I did." She stopped long enough to take a deep breath. "I didn't realize how I was making you feel. I came out here hoping I could *make* you feel that way, but I didn't know you *already* did. If you know what I mean."

"Well, of course I feel that way. Don't you think I miss my real home? And my real friends?"

For the next hour and a half Meg and Molly talked the way both of them should have talked the first day.

"We thought you liked the Kansas kids better," explained Meg.

"Better?" Molly said. "I like them. I like them a lot. They've really made it easier for me to be so far away from you and home. But better? Never."

"We thought you had more fun riding horses than you would being in the club. We thought you thought we were too babyish for you now. We thought — " Meg was unable to finish her sentence because Molly was hugging her too tightly.

"Friends 4-Ever, right?" said Molly into Meg's shoulder. "That's what we'll always, be. That's what we promised."

Then Meg broke away from Molly and a big smile spread across her face. "Molly, I hereby call to order an emergency meeting of the Kansas chapter of the Friends 4-Ever Club." Meg tapped her knuckles on Molly's wall to signal the meeting was about to begin.

Molly laughed. "Meeting? Emergency? What about?"

"I just got my greatest idea since I had the idea to come visit you," Meg said excitedly. "I can't believe how perfect this is going to be."

"What is it?" Molly asked.

Meg shut the door to Molly's room and spent

the next hour explaining her great idea to Molly. Mrs. Quindlen could hear the girls laughing and talking just the way they always used to in Crispin Landing, but she couldn't tell what it was all about. When she finally called them down for supper, the girls looked happy, tired, and like they were up to something.

"What are you two girls planning?" Mrs. Quindlen asked.

"You'll see soon enough." Molly laughed slyly.

Mrs. Quindlen knew the girls well enough to know there was no use trying to get them to tell their secret. They would tell it when they were good and ready.

"You'll find out at the end of the week," Meg teased. "Before I leave you'll know what the secret is."

Molly's mother just looked at them and raised her eyebrows a little. The girls were so busy giggling over their secret plan, they didn't notice the strange smile on Mrs. Quindlen's face. They talked all through dinner about the day's horseback riding lesson, the bee sting, and the next lessons, which Meg said she was ready, willing, and anxious for.

It was an early-to-bed night for the girls, since they had gotten up so early. And for the next few days their routine was much the same as it was the day of the first lesson. Up early, walk over to Tammy's house, take a lesson, come home, and work on their secret plan. Every day Meg sat a little taller in the saddle, as Starry Night and she began to trust each other more. Once her nervousness was gone, Meg was surprised to realize she really liked riding. An even bigger surprise was that she was beginning to like Tammy. She certainly was a good teacher.

On the day of the sixth lesson, one day before the rodeo and two days before Meg was to go home, Meg had her usual lesson. This time Tammy taught her what she would need to know for the opening ceremony of the rodeo. She would follow Molly and Chocolate in the opening parade around the rodeo ring. All the kids in their age group would be leading the parade. It was already planned that Tammy, Kristy, Claire, Maddie, Wayne, Jake, Molly, and even Meg would be first in the line. Meg was finally feeling very excited about the rodeo.

"Well, you're ready for it," Tammy said. "I

can't believe I did it in less than a week, but you'll make it all right."

Meg had to laugh. She was the one who had worked so hard learning all kinds of new things that week, but Tammy was talking as though she had done all the work. Meg didn't even mind. She had gotten used to Tammy's ways. When the lesson was over and Molly and Meg were just getting ready to walk back home, Tammy stopped them.

"Wait here," she said. "I have to get something in the house." She ran inside and was back in a minute with something behind her back.

"Here," she said, holding out a bag decorated with horse stickers. "This is for you. Just a few souvenirs from Kansas."

Meg took the bag, opened it, and smiled broadly when she looked inside.

"What's in it?" Molly asked curiously.

First Meg pulled out a blue ribbon. On it was a picture of a horse and the words "First Place."

"My first ribbon," said Tammy proudly.

Next Meg pulled out a small braid of horse hair tied with a red ribbon.

"From Starry Night's tail," explained Tammy.

Meg reached into the bag and pulled out a small horseshoe.

"That's for good luck in the rodeo tomorrow."

And last there was a picture of Tammy sitting on her horse, Fastback.

"So you'll remember who taught you everything you know," Tammy said, smiling almost shyly. "I thought when I first met you that you'd be one of those Eastern girls who would hate horses and hate riding. But you fooled me. You're almost good."

Meg didn't know what to say. Just as she was about to at least say "Thank you" to Tammy, Starry Night reached her nose forward and nuzzled Meg's neck gently.

"Looks like you've got a friend there." Tammy laughed.

Meg smiled as she looked from Tammy to Molly and back to Tammy. "Yeah," she said softly. "It looks like I've got a *few* friends here."

A RODEO FULL OF
SURPRISES

Meg woke up knowing right away that this was going to be one of the most exciting days of her life. For once when she looked over at Molly's bed, Molly was still in it, and she was still sound asleep.

"Hey, Molly," Meg called softly over to the other bed. "Wake up, it's rodeo day!"

Molly stretched her long legs and her arms before opening her eyes. "Oh," she said yawning widely. "I was just having the best dream. It was all of us, you and Stevie and Laura and me back in Crispin Landing riding our bikes all around your circle."

"You must've dreamed that because of Stevie's letter about the parade," Meg said. "You should be dreaming about riding Chocolate all around the rodeo ring! I'm so excited!"

Now Molly was out of bed and hurrying over to her closet. "Close your eyes," she said to Meg. "I have a surprise for you."

Meg did as she was told. Squeezing her eyes tightly shut she asked, "What is it?" She could hear Molly rustling around in the closet. "Oooo, what is it?" she asked again.

"Okay, open," said Molly. *"Ta-da!"* In each hand Molly held a beautiful satin Western-style shirt, fringe and all. One was red and one was baby blue. "The blue is for you because it matches your eyes," Molly said, handing Meg her new shirt. "My Mom got them for us for the rodeo."

"They're beautiful!" shouted Meg, rushing to try hers on. She put on her freshly washed jeans and her sneakers.

"Wait a minute," Molly said, stopping her from tying her shoe. "There's another surprise." This time she reached in the closet and pulled

126

out a brand-new pair of cowboy boots. They were tan with a dark brown pattern and baby blue leather toe tips. They looked perfect with Meg's shirt.

"Incredible!" shouted Meg. "They're perfect!" She tried them on right away and they fit perfectly. Meg stood up and was immediately two inches taller. She looked in the mirror and liked what she saw. "I look like I was born here," she said, remembering how the model Becky Slade looked in her boots and Western shirt.

Molly stepped in front of the mirror, too. Standing there in her red shirt, jeans, and black cowboy boots with red leather toe tips, she and Meg looked like they belonged together. Meg thought back to all the different photographs in Becky's model portfolio. Becky had looked like so many different people, depending on what she wore. But she was still Becky, no matter what the clothes were.

Meg looked at Molly's reflection and then at her own. We're not really different after all, she thought to herself. Even in their Western rodeo clothes, Meg realized that Molly was still Molly and she was still Meg. They just *looked* different, that was all.

"Don't we look fabulous?" Molly said, turning around to get a good look at the red fringe on the back of her shirt.

"You sure do!" Mrs. Quindlen said. She stood in the doorway, looking at the two girls. "It won't be long before it's time to get over to the fairgrounds for the rodeo. But you two look like you're all ready."

"Oh, Mrs. Quindlen," said Meg, "thank you so, so, so much for the beautiful shirt and boots. They fit perfectly."

"You're welcome, Meg. I couldn't let you ride in your first rodeo without something special to wear, now could I?"

"Let's go show Daddy," Molly said, starting out the door.

"Daddy's gone. He had a special errand to run this morning. But he'll meet us at the rodeo. He'll be there in plenty of time for the opening ceremony. We'll be leaving in about half an hour. Come down and have breakfast before we go." Molly's mother smiled at the girls and then went downstairs to help Scotty and Grandpa get breakfast ready.

Molly fussed with her hair for a minute, then she changed her earrings from small gold balls to her favorite pair, the horseshoes. Meg watched as Molly stuck the thin, gold posts through the holes in her ears and decided again that she could wait a while before having her own ears pierced. While Molly took one last look at herself in the mirror, Meg fluffed up her curls. Molly took one last thing out of the closet, put it in a bag, and they were ready.

The ride to the fairgrounds was short. As Mrs. Quindlen pulled the car into the parking lot, Scotty pointed out all the exciting things he saw to his grandfather. "Look at all the flags, Grandpa! Look at the bull! Did you see those guys doing the lasso? Wow! Look at all the different horses!"

Meg knew how Scotty felt. She was just as excited by all the colorful flags and streamers and ribbons. Hundreds of people were already walking around, looking at the calves that would be roped, the horses that would be ridden, and the cowboy clowns who would be falling off the horses just for fun. It was an incredible sight to see, and Meg couldn't help but wish Stevie and Laura could be there to share it with them.

"Hey, Molly!" Kristy called out of the crowd. "Hurry up, you two. I've got Chocolate and

Starry Night all ready for you. You look great!"

"So do you," said Meg. Kristy wore jeans, bright green cowboy boots, and a bright green satin shirt with yellow fringe on the back. Her hair was in a long braid down her back, with green and yellow ribbons entwined in the braid.

"We'll be a rodeo rainbow!" Molly laughed. The rainbow got even brighter when Tammy in her purple satin shirt, Claire in her orange shirt, Maddie in her yellow shirt, and Jake and Wayne in their royal blue shirts all joined the girls. Everyone exchanged excited greetings as they did last-minute fussing over their horses.

"Now you remember everything I told you, right?" Tammy said to Meg.

"I hope so," Meg said, feeling nervous. What if she fell off the horse?

"You'll be great, Meg," Molly assured her. "And our surprise is going to be even greater."

"What surprise?" asked Kristy, noticing the bag Molly was carrying.

"You'll see when we start the ceremony," Molly said. Suddenly she remembered her father. "Gosh, I hope my Dad gets here in time." She looked up into the stands, where the audience would be sitting. She could see her mother and Scotty and Grandpa. They had great seats, right in the middle. Molly could see that her mother was saving a space next to her, but her father wasn't there yet.

"Ladies and gentlemen, may I have your attention please?" The announcer's voice filled the fairgrounds and a hush fell over the crowd. "Will the riders in the opening ceremony please take your places on your horses. We will stand for the singing of our National Anthem."

Molly, Meg, Kristy, and the rest of the riders in their group mounted their horses. Starry Night stood perfectly still for Meg as she climbed up. Once she was settled, Molly passed something to Meg and gave her the OK sign with her thumb and index finger forming a circle. Meg signaled OK back. The crowd stood up and the riders stood still as the recorded music began. Meg looked around and could hardly believe she was really there, sitting on a horse and getting ready to ride in front of all these strangers! She looked across the standing crowd of people and easily found Mrs. Quindlen. She saw Scotty. She saw Grandpa. And then what she saw she couldn't believe.

"Molly!" she whispered loudly.

Molly looked over at her and shushed her with a finger to her lips.

"Look!" Meg whispered excitedly, pointing over to the stands. "Your father is back. And look who's with him!"

Molly looked. The sun was in her eyes, so she held her hand up to shade them. Then she saw what Meg was so excited about. "It's Stevie! And Laura!" Molly exclaimed. The music ended just as Molly was about to scream out to them, but they screamed out to her first.

"Molly!" Stevie was shouting from her place in the stands.

"Meg!" Laura yelled, waving her arms to make sure her friends saw her.

"Ladies and gentlemen," the announcer boomed, "Cross Plains is proud to present her finest young riders in the opening ceremony of this Rodeo Round-up. Let's give them a big hand as they start off the events of the day."

The crowds screamed and shouted and whistled and stomped their feet as Tammy led the parade, followed by Kristy, Claire, Maddie, Wayne, Jake, Molly, and Meg. When Molly was almost in front of where her family with Stevie and Laura were sitting, she suddenly held up her half of a long blue banner. It stretched between her and Meg, and painted in bright yellow letters were the words, "Molly, Meg, Laura, Stevie, and all the Kansas Kids — Friends 4-Ever!"

This surprise banner drew cheers from everyone, but no one felt happier at this moment than Meg Milano. She saw Tammy turn around to see what the extra screams were about, and a big smile spread across Tammy's face when she read the banner. In fact, the banner was such a success that the opening ceremony riders were asked to ride around the arena two extra times so that everyone could get a good look at it.

When at last Tammy led her parade out of the arena, Stevie, Laura, and the Quindlens were already down from the stands. Kristy held Chocolate for Molly and Tammy held Starry Night for Meg while the two girls buried themselves in hugs and kisses and shouts from Stevie and Laura.

"How did you get here?" Molly demanded.

"I can't believe this!" Meg cried. "I just wished for this and now it came true!"

"We just called an emergency meeting," explained Stevie, "and decided that instead of going to day camp we'd come here instead."

"This was a little surprise we worked out with Stevie's mother and the Ryders," Mrs. Quindlen added. "You can't be the only ones planning secret surprises you know." They all laughed, but stopped long enough for Molly to introduce her Crispin Landing friends to her Kansas friends. They would all have plenty of time to get to know each other better. The girls would be staying another week.

"Well," said Tammy, looking at Stevie and Laura, "I guess I can get you two riding in a week. It won't be easy, but I'll manage."

Stevie and Laura weren't quite sure how to take what Tammy had said. But Meg just went over to the red-haired girl and gave her a big hug. "You'll manage, all right," Meg laughed.

The four Friends 4-Ever Club members spent the rest of the rodeo day cheering for their Kansas friends as they rode and roped and raced in the other events. And that night, tired but still excited, Meg, Molly, Laura, and Stevie settled into beds and roll-away cots in Molly's room.

Meg knocked her knuckles on Molly's desk.

"Uh-oh," laughed Stevie. "I guess we know what's coming now."

"I now call this emergency club meeting officially to order," Meg announced.

"Emergency?" said Laura and Molly together.

"Now what's the problem?" Stevie said, rolling her eyes up.

"No problem," said Meg, smiling at her best friends. "No problem at all." Meg knocked her knuckles on the desk again and said, "Meeting adjourned. Over, finished, and done!"

"Hooray!" cheered Stevie.

"Three cheers for Meg," added Laura.

"And a million cheers for the best best friends anyone could ever have," Molly finished.

It was just the way it used to be at the sleepovers they had had in Crispin Landing. Stevie's bed was lined up right next to Molly's, and Meg and Laura had their beds head to head so they could whisper long into the night without waking anyone. Meg and Molly made Stevie and Laura tell again and again how all the plans were worked out so they could come to Kansas, too.

"We couldn't stand it one second longer," Stevie was saying. "The Friends 4-Ever Club belongs together. If you couldn't come to us, Molly, then we just had to come to you."

"And so here we are," said Laura happily. "All together again, just the way it always was."

"And the way it always will be," added Meg. "We may not always be able to be right next to each other, but nothing can keep us from writing and talking to each other."

"Nothing except sleep," yawned Stevie, closing her tired eyes.

"Umm," Laura agreed. "Sleep sounds good to me." It had been a long day and they had traveled a long way. In another minute Laura and Stevie had both drifted off into a deep sleep.

Meg looked across to Molly's bed. "Molly?" she said quietly. "Are you still awake?"

"Uh-huh," Molly whispered back through the darkness. Her eyes were closed, too.

"I'm glad you're happy here," Meg said.

"And I'm glad *you're* here. I'm glad you're *all* here." As Molly, too, fell asleep, she realized that for the first time in almost a whole year she really felt at home in Kansas. The room was different. The house was different. But with Laura, Stevie, and Meg there beside her, the feelings of home were very much the same.

"Molly?" Meg whispered again. But this time there was no answer. Meg was just as tired as the rest, but thinking kept her awake. As she looked around the room at the other three club members, Meg got an idea. Quietly she climbed out of bed and went to her tote bag for a piece of stationery and a pen. By the light of the hallway, with only Riggs watching, Meg wrote:

Dear Molly,
    No matter where
    No matter how far,
    Friends 4-Ever
    Is what we all are.
                Love,

      Meg, Stevie, and Laura

Meg climbed back into bed, closed her eyes, and was soon asleep with the rest of the Friends 4-Ever.

WIN A <u>FRIENDSHIP</u> NECKLACE

Enter the **Friends 4-Ever™** Giveaway!

From "Yours Truly" to "Yours 'Til the Meatball Bounces", there are so many ways to sign-off your letters...

WHAT IS YOUR FAVORITE LETTER SIGN-OFF?

Tell us your favorite sign-off and you may win a "Best Friends" friendship necklace! It's really two necklaces with a heart pendant broken into two pieces — one for you and one for your best friend! Just fill in the coupon below and return by November 30, 1990.

Rules: Entries must be postmarked by November 30, 1990. Winners will be picked at random and notified by mail. No purchase necessary. Void where prohibited. Taxes on prizes are the responsibility of the winners and their immediate families. Employees of Scholastic Inc.; its agencies, affiliates, subsidiaries; and their immediate families not eligible. For a complete list of winners, send a self-addressed stamped envelope to Friends 4-Ever Giveaway, Giveaway Winners List, at the address provided below.

Fill in the coupon below or write the information on a 3" x 5" piece of paper and mail to: **FRIENDS 4-EVER GIVEAWAY,** Scholastic Inc., P.O. Box 753, 730 Broadway, New York, NY 10003. Canadian residents send entries to: Iris Ferguson, Scholastic Inc., 123 Newkirk Road, Richmond Hill, Ontario, Canada L4C365.

100 Winners!

Friends 4-Ever Giveaway

My favorite sign-off is:

_____

Name _____ Age_____

Street _____

City_____ State_____ Zip_____

Where did you buy this *Friends 4-Ever* book?

❑ Bookstore ❑ Drugstore ❑ Supermarket ❑ Library

❑ Book Club ❑ Book Fair ❑ Other_____(specify) FF290

#5 SEALED WITH A HUG

Why is Molly acting so strange?

Molly's back for the holidays ...but Crispin Landing just isn't the same! Her house, the town — *everything* seems so different! Meg, Laura, and Stevie are sure it'll be just like old times — caroling, tree decorating, and cookie baking! But all Molly talks about is her new friend and how wonderful country life is in Kansas!

Are Meg, Laura, and Stevie losing Molly's friendship... 4-ever?

Available October wherever you buy books!

FF290